D0386644

WITHDRAWN

the gangster we are all looking for

YOLO COUNTY LIBRARY
226 BUCKEYE STREET
WOODLAND, CA 95695

lê thi diem thúy

the gangster we are all looking for

Alfred A. Knopf New York 2003

This Is a Borzoi Book Published by Alfred A. Knopf

Copyright © 2003 by lê thi diem thúy

All rights reserved under International and Pan-American Copyright Conventions.
Published in the United States by Alfred A. Knopf, a division of Random House, Inc.,
New York, and simultaneously in Canada by Random House of Canada Limited,
Toronto. Distributed by Random House, Inc., New York.

www.aaknopf.com

Portions of this work originally appeared in *Harper's Magazine*, *The Massachusetts Review*, and *The Best American Essays* (Boston: Houghton Mifflin, 1999).

Knopf, Borzoi Books, and the colophon are registered trademarks
of Random House, Inc.

Library of Congress Cataloging-in-Publication Data
lê, thi diem thúy, 1972–
The gangster we are all looking for / lê thi diem thúy.— 1st ed.
p. cm.
ISBN 0-375-40018-4
1. Vietnamese American families—Fiction. 2. Vietnamese American
children—Fiction. 3. Vietnamese Americans—Fiction. 4. San Diego (Calif.)—
Fiction. 5. Refugees—Fiction. 6. Girls—Fiction. I. Title.
PS3612.E2 G36 2003
813'.6—dc21   2002033999

Manufactured in the United States of America
First Edition

For my family, near and far,
and in memory of Nguyen Thi My

In Vietnamese, the word for *water* and the word for *a nation, a country,* and *a homeland* are one and the same: *nu'ó'c*.

contents

the gangster we are all looking for

suh·top!

Linda Vista, with its rows of yellow houses, is where we eventually washed to shore. Before Linda Vista, we lived in the Green Apartment on Thirtieth and Adams, in Normal Heights. Before the Green Apartment, we lived in the Red Apartment on Forty-ninth and Orange, in East San Diego. Before the Red Apartment we weren't a family like we are a family now. We were in separate places, waiting for each other. Ma was standing on a beach in Vietnam while Ba and I were in California with four men who had escaped with us on the same boat.

Ba and I were connected to the four uncles, not by blood but by water. The six of us had stepped into the South China Sea together. Along with other people from our town, we floated across the sea, first in the hold of the fishing boat, and then in the hold of a U.S. Navy ship. At the refugee camp in Singapore, we slept on beds side by side and when our papers were processed and stamped, we packed our few possessions and left the camp together. We entered the revolving doors of airports and boarded plane after plane. We were lifted high over the Pacific Ocean. Holding on to one another, we moved through clouds, ghost vapors, time zones. On the other side, we walked through a light rain and climbed into a car together. We were carried through unfamiliar brightly lit streets, and delivered to the sidewalk in front of a darkened house whose door we entered, after climbing five uneven steps together in what had become pouring rain.

In 1978, an elderly couple in San Diego decided to sponsor, through their church group, five young Vietnamese men and one six-year-old girl from a refugee camp in Singapore. Mr. Russell was a retired Navy man. He had once been stationed in the Pacific and remembered the people there as being small and kind. When Mr. Russell heard about the Vietnamese boat people, he spent many sleepless nights staring at the ceiling and thinking about the nameless, faceless bodies lying in small boats, floating on the open water. In Mr. Russell's mind, the Vietnamese boat people merged with his memories of the Okinawans and the Samoans and even the Hawaiians.

One night, Mr. Russell fell asleep and dreamed that the boats were seabirds sitting on the waves. He saw a hand scoop the birds up from the water. It was not his hand and it was not the hand of God.

The birds went flying in all directions across the blinding blue sky of Mr. Russell's dream, but finally he saw them fly in only one direction and that was toward the point where in the dream he understood himself to be waiting, somewhere beyond the frame.

The original plan was that my father, the four uncles and I would live with the elderly couple, but as our papers were being processed Mr. Russell died and there was some question as to where we would be sent. Tokyo? Sydney? Minneapolis?

Mr. Russell had told Mrs. Russell his dream about the birds. After his death, she considered the dream and decided that we should move in with their son, Melvin.

Ba said it was no one's fault that we lasted only one season at Mel's place.

When Mel approached us at the airport, we heard a faint rattling: a ring full of gold and silver keys hanging from his belt. With each step Mel took, the ring swung and rattled by his side. The keys were new to him. Mel was tall and thin, but the ring looked fat, important. Mel caught the ring and pushed it into his pocket. This silenced the keys for a moment. He shook everyone's hand—

including mine—and laughing nervously said, "Welcome to America."

He then waved his hand in the air and when I followed it with my eyes, I saw a poster of a man and a woman at the beach, lying on striped towels, sunning themselves between two tall palm trees. Above the palm trees were large block letters that looked like they were on fire: SUNNY SAN DIEGO. The man was lying on his stomach, his face buried in his folded arms. The woman was lying on her back, with one leg down and the other leg up, bent at the knee. I looked through the triangle formed by the woman's tanned knee, calf and thigh and saw the calm, sleeping waves of the ocean. My mother was out there somewhere. My father had said so.

After Mel and his mother took us to the room in Mel's house where Ba, the four uncles and I would all be sleeping, they wished us goodnight and left us alone, closing the door quietly behind them. They stood in the hallway and we could hear them talking. Even without understanding a word of what they were saying, the tone of their voices troubled us. Had we been able to understand, we might have heard the following:

"I feel like I've inherited a boatload of people. I mean, I've been living here alone and now I've got five men I've never met before, and what about that little girl?"

"Dear, you know your father wanted them here."

"Here in America, sure, but not here with me."

"Well, it's worked out that way. If your father were here—"

The woman started to cry.

"I'm sorry, Mother. I'm so sorry."

We heard their footsteps move down the hallway toward the living room.

Inside the bedroom, we all remained quiet in our places. Ba was standing with his back against the door. The four men were sitting on the two bunk beds and I was sitting on the double bed, my knees pulled up near my chest.

One of the uncles took a deep breath and lay down on the bed. He was still wearing his shoes and let his feet hang off the edge of the bed so he wouldn't get the covers dirty.

Ba stepped forward and explained to the four men and me that Mel had bought our way into the United States. He said that Mel was a good man. We heard without really listening. We nodded. Ba said that Mel had let the people at the airport gates know that it was O.K. for us to be here. "If it wasn't for him," Ba said, "they would have sent us back the way we came."

We each thought of those long nights floating on the ocean, rocking back and forth in the middle of nowhere with nothing in sight. We remembered the ships that kept their distance. We remembered the people leaning over the decks of the ships to study us through their binoculars and not liking what they saw, turning away from our boat. If it was true that this man Mel could keep us from floating back there—to those salt-filled nights—what could we do but thank him. And then thank him again. Only why did it seem from the tones of the voices in the hallway as if something was wrong?

Ba said that we had to be patient.

Two of the uncles nodded. One closed his eyes. One lay down and turned toward the wall. I wrapped my arms around my knees and studied my bare feet. They were very clean; not a speck of sand or salt on them.

Ba said whatever we might come to think of Mel, we should always remember that he opened a door for us and that this was an important thing to remember.

There were things about us Mel never knew or remembered. He didn't remember that we hadn't come running through the door he opened but, rather, had walked, keeping close together and moving very slowly, as people often do when they have no idea what they're walking toward or what they're walking from. And he never knew that during our first night in America, as he and his mother sat on the living room couch holding on to each other and crying because Mr. Russell was gone, Ba had climbed out the bedroom window and was sitting in the shadow of the palm trees on the front lawn of the house, staring at the moon like a lost dog, and also crying.

. . .

The ring of gold and silver keys that rattled beside Mel opened the doors to condominiums, duplexes, and town houses in various states of neglect. Mel was not good with tools and, since a bicycle accident in early childhood, was generally rather fearful, a fact that had always pained him, especially around his father. In exchange for letting us live with him—an arrangement he reluctantly agreed to, to satisfy what his mother called his father's "dying wish"— Mel employed Ba and the four uncles as his crew of house painters and general maintenance men. He was relieved not to have to climb shaky ladders or crawl through dark, narrow spaces to see about small broken things.

When the white walls in one of his properties had faded or become dirty with the grubby prints of people's lives rubbing up against them, he sent Ba and the four uncles in with directions to "touch them up," "make like new," "make white again."

On almost every day of the week, you could find them working: five small-boned Vietnamese men climbing ladders in empty rooms, painting the white walls whiter.

"So much white is unlucky."

"Layers of white bury you."

"In between the first coat and the third—"

"Death could slip in and—"

"Press you up against the wall and—"

"Wrap you up in coats of white."

"Dressing you for your own funeral."

.　.　.

Of all the men, Ba knew the most English; he had picked some up from the Americans during the war. The uncles asked Ba to ask Mel why the walls had to be so white. Ba didn't know the word "so." His question came out like this:

"Why white?"

Mel said, "It's clean."

That was the end of the conversation.

When Ba told the uncles what Mel had said, they stared at him blankly.

"No," they said, turning to the white walls. "We don't understand."

They picked up their paintbrushes and rollers and rags and went back to work.

Ba tried to tell them again, the way Mel had told him, in that voice that shines bright in your face like a flashlight aimed at your eyes when you're sleeping. It's a voice that doesn't explain, though it often says things in tones that make you wonder. My Ba does not have such a voice. Ba's voice echoes from deep down like a frog singing at the bottom of a well. His voice is water moving through a reed pipe in the middle of a sad tune. And the sad voice is always asking and answering itself. It calls out and then comes running in. It is the tide of my Ba's mind. When I listen to it, I can see boats floating around in his head. Boats full of people trying to get somewhere.

.   .   .

Mel had stopped going to church years ago but after his father's death, he started going again. Every Sunday morning he would drive to his parents' house to pick up his mother and accompany her to church. During our first month at Mel's, Ba and the four uncles and I would all pile into the car and go with them. But after a couple of Sundays in a row during which the uncles either slept through the sermon or stared at the floor absentmindedly, picking dried paint off their hands and fingernails, it was decided that we should stay at the house while Mel and his mother went to church.

After church, Mel would bring his mother by to visit with us.

We would all gather around the coffee table in the living room, Mel seated on the lounge chair in the corner, reading the Sunday paper, Ba, the four uncles and I taking turns smiling at Mrs. Russell, who sat on the couch and smiled patiently back at us.

"Now, what's happening in the world?" she'd ask Mel.

"Oh, the usual," he'd answer.

Mrs. Russell's face was always made up, and when I leaned in reluctantly to kiss her, it smelled of sweet powder and rouge. She wore necklaces and earrings with bright purple and red stones. Some of the earrings were in the shape of flowers and some hung like clusters of lights shining from either side of her face.

From that house of bachelors, Mrs. Russell chose my Ba and me as her favorites. Perhaps she sensed we'd once had a woman in our lives. She bought me pastel-colored dresses to wear to school and smaller versions of those necklaces and earrings she liked to wear. The jewelry came cushioned on cotton squares inside little white boxes that rattled hollow when she shook them.

On Sunday afternoons that first winter, she would take my Ba and me for long drives up into the mountains. After the telephone wires and the streets of the city had slowly given way to treetops and gravel roads, we would get out of the car and find ourselves surrounded by snow. A small woods stood before us, and the road fell away in the distance behind us. There was nothing up there but snow and sky. And it seemed that all we ever did was walk in circles, making footprints in the soft snow.

After the third trip to the mountain, I asked Ba why Mel's mother was always taking us up to the snow.

He said, "Maybe she thinks we think it's magic, the way she can take us to a snowy place that's so near a hot city."

"Why doesn't she take us to the beach?" I asked.

Ba shook his head. "No. Not possible. There's no reason for us to go there."

"But Ma's there," I said.

"No, she's not," Ba said, leaning down to zip up my jacket.

"You told me she was at the beach," I said.

"Not the beach here. The beach in Vietnam," Ba said.

What was the difference?

The grandmother brought a small camera with her on these trips. She liked looking at things through it. On our very first trip to the mountain, she took a photograph of Ba and me standing in front of Mel's blue car.

In the photograph, Ba is wearing brown pants and a turquoise velour sweatshirt. His hair is parted on the side and pushed back behind one ear. I am wearing blue jeans and a yellow-and-red striped sweater that you can't see because it's under the ivory-colored sweater the grandmother had pulled from the trunk of the car, shaking the dust off before helping me into it. Before we took this picture Ba brushed my bangs across my forehead so they wouldn't fall in my eyes.

In this photograph, my Ba and I hold hands and lean against the blue car. We are looking at the camera, waiting for that flash that lets us know something has happened inside the body of the camera, something that makes it remember us, remember our faces, remember our clothes, remember the blurred shape of our hands captured in that second when we shivered, waiting.

After the grandmother took this picture, she led us toward the woods.

. . .

That first day on the mountain, I made a game of following in my Ba's footsteps so I left no tracks of my own in the snow. When I stopped and looked back in the direction we had come from, I could see only my Ba's footprints and the grandmother's. The footprints began at the car, which looked, from a distance, like a shining blue box that had dropped from the sky.

I watched Ba walking slowly toward the woods. He had his hands behind his back and was staring at the ground. The grandmother walked ahead of him. She was looking through her camera at the sky, at the tops of trees and, sometimes, back at us.

I ran after them.

In the thickest part of the woods, she stopped walking and turned to face us. She was smiling and I remember how her head shook slightly, sending the shiny balls on her earlobes swinging like searchlights.

She laid her palm against the trunk of a tree and with her finger traced some letters that had been carved there. She was smiling and crying at the same time.

I closed my eyes. When I opened them, Ba was squatting in the snow with his eyes closed and his hands to his ears the way I used to squat in the shadow of the fishing boats at home when we played hide-and-go-seek, my eyes shut tight so no one could see me. I ran over to Ba and threw my arms around his neck and climbed onto his back.

"Where's my Ba?" I asked, pretending he was a big rock. "I wonder where my Ba is hiding in all this snow."

The big rock stood up and became a tree. The tree tried to shake off all the snow that had gathered on its branches. I held on tightly and the tree became a wild horse whose neck I clung to as it went running across the fields. The horse ran and ran and ran. And as it ran, it asked itself, "I wonder where my little girl has disappeared to."

I put my hands in front of my Ba's eyes and wiggled my fingers like ten squirming fish out of water. I said, "Ba! Ba! Here I am! I'm right here!"

We galloped out of the woods, stamping designs into the snow. We shouted each other's names and let them echo all around. Out of the corner of my eye, I saw the woods getting smaller. When Ba stopped running to catch his breath, I heard the light crunching of the grandmother's steps, somewhere far behind us.

Ba and I envied the four uncles. They were never invited to come with us on the mountain drives. They spent their Sunday afternoons walking around the neighborhood, looking for signs of other Vietnamese people. It took them a while but they finally found some other Vietnamese men at a pool hall. Every Sunday after that, they would return to the pool hall.

While Ba and I were following the grandmother around in the snow, the uncles were smoking cigarettes, drinking iced coffee, shooting pool and learning to watch and then bet on football games with their new Vietnamese brothers. They had such a good time they wouldn't come home until late on Sunday nights. Ba and I would wake up early on Monday mornings and find the uncles asleep on their bunk beds.

Often they would still have their coats on and one uncle, sleeping on a top bunk, never managed to kick off both his shoes. Ba would lift me up and I would wiggle the shoe from side to side until I could pull it off the uncle's foot. Then I would fish under the bed for the shoe that had been kicked off the night before. I would pair the shoes and leave them in the middle of the room, with their toes pointing toward the door.

Weekday mornings, after I'd brushed my teeth and washed my face, Ba would hand me one of the pastel-colored dresses the grandmother had given me. I'd pull the itchy, rustling dress over my head and let it hang for a moment around my neck, a huge flower whose petals were bunched and whose center had been replaced by my frowning face.

"I don't want to wear American dresses," I'd say to Ba.

Ba lowered the edges of his mouth and raised his eyebrows at the same time, like a clown about to cry. He shrugged his shoulders at me and reached under the bed for my school shoes, a pair of clear plastic sandals—also from the grandmother—that let the playground pebbles get stuck between my toes every time I kicked at the dirt.

I'd run around the room and let the dress rise up

and down around my neck, like rooster feathers ruffling before a cockfight.

"Who wants to wear American dresses? Who?" Running in small circles I'd chant a litany of "Who? Who? Who?"

Ba would sometimes join me by standing on one leg and kicking back with the other, with his hands cupped under his armpits and his elbows jutting out like wings. Tilting his head to one side, he'd furrow his brow and chant, "Who? Who? Who?"

"Who's there?" one of the uncles would ask, in a sleepy voice.

I'd run out of the room pulling the dress on in the hallway. From inside the room, I could hear Ba's voice, reassuring. "It was only the girl, dancing."

"Cooing like a common pigeon," another of the uncles would complain.

"Every morning that girl runs around like a headless chicken," said another.

"Isn't she late for school?" asked yet another.

I'd stand in the hallway, leaning casually against the wall, my legs crossed at the ankles. After a minute, Ba would come out of the room, quietly closing the door behind him. He'd hand me my plastic sandals. I'd sit down on the floor of the hallway and slip them on. As I tightened the buckles, I could hear the uncles rolling around in their beds, groaning, trying to find the comfortable spot they'd lost upon waking.

Ba and I would tiptoe to the front door. Mel often slept until noon, so we all had to be quiet when leaving the house.

We'd stand on the sidewalk and Ba would comb my hair with his fingers. Then he'd pull two barrettes out of his shirt pocket, push my hair away from my eyes, and gently snap the barrettes in place.

As we walked toward the school, he'd often tell me not to make so much noise in the morning.

Once, he told me Mel had complained to him that he could hear me "chattering in his sleep." When Ba told me that, I said, "Dumb birds chatter. I don't chatter." Ba squeezed my hand and didn't say anything.

A block away from my school, Ba and I would stop at a red-and-white sign on the street corner and I'd put my arm around the post. We did this every morning. Ba would stand beside me and wait while I then wrapped one leg around the post and hung my head as far as it would go to one side.

I liked looking at things from this angle. Everything was upside down. I would look at the long gray chain-link fence that surrounded my school playground. I imagined how all the children standing with their feet pressed firmly against the ground, and their heads pointing toward the top of the chain-link fence, would slowly slip into the pale blue sky. I imagined the children floating, their dresses ballooning out around them as the wind ruffled their hair across their faces. I'd look over at Ba, also upside down, and I would imagine him floating too, with his hands folded across his chest.

While the blood was rushing to my head, Ba was studying the letters on the sign. He practiced reading the word. He would slowly part his lips and then close them, making this sound: "Suh-top!" "Suh-top!" "Suh-top!"

I was the only Vietnamese student at my school. On the first day of class, the teacher introduced me to the other students by holding a globe in one hand as she gave it a spin with the other, and then pointing with her finger at an S-shaped curve near a body of water.

Was that where I had come from?

As I stood before them in a dress the color of an Easter egg, with my feet encased in clear plastic sandals, the other students looked at the globe and then back at me again. Some whispered behind their hands. Some just stared. I imagined the stripes on my underwear flashing on and off, like traffic signals, under the dress.

At recess that first day of school, as I stood in the shadow of a big electrical box on the edge of the playground, I missed my older brother. Could he see me standing here? Was he wondering why I wasn't playing with the other children? Wasn't I exactly like our limp-footed schoolmaster in Vietnam? The one who used to stand in the doorway of the schoolhouse and watch his students run up and down the beach yelling,

"Hey! Who can run faster than me?"

"Who can jump higher than this?"

"Who can swim past the horizon and back before the end of recess?"

When the loud bell rang at the end of recess the students at my American school formed a line at the edge of the blacktop. In a line, my class walked into a big room with rows of plastic green mats on the floor. The mats were in groups of two or three, separated by shelves of children's toys. Everyone lay down on a mat with eyes shut until we were given a signal to open our eyes again.

"Go to sleep now," the teacher would say. "If you can't sleep, close your eyes and try to rest. Close your eyes. That will help."

Ever since my brother left, I've had a hard time taking naps. At school in America, I lay on the green mat and stared at the white ceiling. Sometimes I would see a blond baby doll lying beside me on the shelf of toys. I would entangle my fingers in her coarse hair and lie still, listening to the other students breathe. While the doll's blue eyes were dutifully closed behind long brown lashes, I stared at the ceiling and studied the shapes I saw there: a chair, a tree trunk, the worried face of an old man, a sliver of moon.

I began to play with the ceiling, a game that I used to play with the sky when I was lying in the fishing boat on the sea. At that time, I thought that everyone and everything I missed was hovering behind the sky. The game involved looking for a seam to the sky, a thread I could pull. I told myself that if I could find the thread and focus on it hard enough with my eyes, I could tear the sky open and my mother, my brother, my grandfather, my flip-flops, my favorite shells, would all fall down to me.

Before I could find the thread that would split the ceiling wide open, a student wearing a cape and holding a silver stick with a shiny star at its tip would come around to wake us. The star-holder shuffled quietly among the sleeping bodies, touching the star to one after another. The sleeping students stirred and woke. But when the star-holder came to wake me, I always sat up before he could touch me. Once, I forgot that my fingers were still entangled in the doll's hair. As I sat up, her body jerked forward with me, knocking the plastic fruit off the shelf. Apples and oranges bounced onto the floor. That day, the star-holder hurried past me.

"Shhhh!" My teacher said, pressing a long finger against her fish lips. "Shhhh!"

Over the years, Mr. and Mrs. Russell had collected small glass figures of animals, mainly horses. The animals had skinny glass legs you could see through, as through a clean window. After Mr. Russell's death, Mrs. Russell decided that her son Melvin should have some of these glass animals, along with a number of other things that had once belonged to his father.

One Sunday afternoon Mel and his mother pulled up to the house and Mel called for Ba and the uncles to come out and help him. A glass display cabinet was wedged in the open trunk of Mel's car. After directing a couple of the uncles to maneuver the cabinet carefully out of the trunk, Mel told Ba and the other uncles to get the three cardboard boxes sitting on the backseat and then he waved for everyone to follow him. With his mother holding the front door open, Mel led the uncles and Ba up the five uneven steps and into the house. They carried the cabinet and the three boxes down the long hallway and around to the back of the house, to a room that was Mel's office. I followed behind them, my hands tucked in the back pockets of my jeans.

Mel's office was a small and crowded room. Half-emptied boxes lay on the floor. Shelves bowing under the weight of books and files lined the walls, and in the center of the room was a large square desk, its top covered with pens, papers, receipt books, a tray of keys and spare change. Behind the desk was a leather swivel chair.

Mel directed the uncles to place the glass cabinet in the far corner of the room, so that while sitting at his desk, he could look up and see into the cabinet.

As we stood watching, Mel and his mother unpacked the contents of the three cardboard boxes and placed them carefully inside the glass cabinet. First we saw five pieces of blue-and-white china. Then came some red leather-bound books. Mel spun the wheels on a toy fire truck before placing it inside the cabinet. His mother unwrapped a pipe that still had tobacco in it and handed it to Mel. Mel lay the pipe down on its side gingerly. The last to come out were the glass animals. There were about twenty of them and they were lined up in pairs, like animals in a parade.

We were invited to look into the glass cabinet. As we stood peering in at the contents, the old woman told Mel to tell Ba to tell the four uncles and me that the things inside were not for touching.

Ba didn't tell us anything; he just asked us, "Do you understand?" and the four uncles and I said, "Yes." We had all sensed that the things in the cabinet were valuable, not because they looked valuable to us but because they had been separated from the disorder of the rest of the room and the rest of the house.

As we were leaving Mel's office, I noticed a golden brown butterfly lying atop some papers on his desk. I reached to touch it. Instead of the powder that usually comes off of butterfly wings, my fingers brushed across cold glass. Pausing in the doorway, I glanced over my shoulder toward the desk. What was that?

. . .

At the beginning and the end of every school day, two older students stood in the middle of the street across from the school entrance; they carried signs they crossed like sabers in battle. This meant the cars—all of them, every one of them, even the big yellow buses—had to stop so the children could cross the street to go to school or cross the street to leave school and go home, wherever home might be.

Each afternoon I would run past the crossed signs to meet whichever uncle had come to walk me back to Mel's house. As the uncle and I passed the red-and-white sign at which Ba and I paused every morning, I'd brush my fingers against the post and whisper, "Hi."

The uncle would let me into the house and I would race down the hallway to our room and change out of the itchy dress into my jeans and a T-shirt. I usually had an hour alone before Ba or one of the other uncles would come home and start dinner.

At first I used to spend the hour coloring or studying the reading book with pictures of the boy, the girl, and their dog, Spot, who liked to chase after the bouncing ball. But after the day we had watched Mel fill his cabinet, I would sneak into Mel's office and spend the hour visiting with the butterfly and the glass animals.

The butterfly was golden brown and I found it lying as before inside the thick glass disk atop the stack of letters and rent receipts on Mel's desk. When I picked up the disk, I saw that the butterfly was trapped in a pool of yellow jelly. Though I turned the glass disk around and around, I could not find the place where the butterfly had flown in or where it could push its way out again.

I held the disk up to my ear and listened. At first all I heard was the sound of my own breathing, but then I heard a soft rustling, like wings brushing against a windowpane. The rustling was a whispered song. It was the butterfly's way of speaking, and I thought I understood it.

I cupped the disk in my palms and, gazing down at the butterfly, carried it over to the window overlooking the back garden. When I held it up to the sunlight, the disk glowed a dazzling yellow and at the center of the yellow was the rich earthen brown shape of the butterfly.

I carried the disk back to the desk and put it back atop the stack of letters and rent receipts. It pressed down on the paper the same way my Ba's heavy head pressed down on the pillow at night, full of thoughts that dragged him into nightmares when all he wanted was a dream as sweet and happy as the taste of jackfruit ice cream.

When Ba and I lay down to sleep one night, I whispered into Ba's ear, "I found a butterfly that has a problem."

"What is the problem?" Ba asked.

"The butterfly is alive . . ."

"Good," Ba said.

"But it's trapped."

"Where?"

"Inside a glass disk."

Ba said nothing.

"But it wants to get out."

"How do you know?"

"Because it said this to me: 'Shuh-shuh/shuh-shuh.' "

Ba sat up, shook his heavy head back and forth and tapped on the side of one ear, then the other.

"What are you doing?" I asked him.

"I must get these butterfly words out of my head before they grow bigger," Ba said, tilting his head far to one side so the words could slip out like water.

"Ahhh . . ." he sighed, pulling on his earlobes, "empty of all butterflies. Now I can sleep."

The next morning, I went out to where the uncles were working, in a corner of the back garden. They were trimming plants, pulling up weeds, refilling the bird feeder. When one of the uncles asked me why I looked so serious, I told him that I needed his help. All the uncles stopped what they were doing and wanted to know what was wrong.

I explained with my fingers arching and meeting in an imperfect circle that there was a butterfly trapped inside a glass disk, and that when you held the disk up to the light—my arms now reaching toward the sun—the butterfly lit up, golden brown.

I asked the uncles to help me get the butterfly out.

"Impossible!"

"That butterfly got itself into a lot of trouble flying into a disk."

"It's not trouble we can do much about, though."

"Yeah, what do we know about butterflies stuck in glass. I never saw anything like it in Vietnam."

"But doesn't it sound terrible?" I asked.

"It must be dead now, that butterfly."

"Can't do much for a dead butterfly."

"No, I heard it rustle its wings. It wants to get out!"

"Listen to me, little girl, no butterfly could stay alive inside a glass disk. Even if its body was alive, I'm sure that butterfly's soul has long since flown away."

"Yes, that's how I think of it also. No soul in that glass disk."

"If there's no soul, how can the butterfly cry for help?" I asked.

"But what does crying mean in this country? Your Ba cries in the garden every night and nothing comes of it."

"Just water for Mel's lawn."

"Nothing."

They went back to work.

The crying butterfly had once flown, but the glass animals lined up side by side on the shelves of Mel's display cabinet had never run anywhere. They never had thick, heavy hooves, the kind that kick up dust and leave deep prints in the muddy banks of rivers. They never kicked at anything or bit anyone, even playfully. They never rubbed their bodies against a tree trunk or rolled on the ground with their legs whipping at the air. These glass animals had legs I could see through and small glass mouths that never opened to eat or drink. They never slept. Their legs didn't bend. Their manes were brittle. The slightest breeze would blow these glass animals onto their sides, and unless I set them right, they would remain that way forever. They were the dumbest animals I had ever met.

When I went into Mel's office, I would open the glass doors of the cabinet and leave them open so the animals could get some air. I always touched the animals. I carried them to the windowsill and let them sit on the sunny ledge, beside my golden butterfly. I told the glass animals stories. I told them about the pigeons that lived atop Lady Six's house. Squatting on the floor of Mel's office, I mimicked the way the pigeons sat on the edge of the roof, waiting to pick at the clumps of day-old rice Lady Six tossed into her courtyard. I stood and made the sound of the pigeons swooping toward the rice. I told them about the roosters that would run along the beach with me, leaving strange scratches in the wet sand. I took a pen and a piece of paper from Mel's desk and drew the rooster alphabet for the glass animals to see. I told the animals how Ma had promised me that when I was old enough, I could take the train into the city with her and she would show me around the big market. I explained that the market was bigger than the cabinet that they lived in, bigger than Mel's house, bigger than the back garden.

I told the glass animals about a picture of the boat that my Ba and the four uncles and I had escaped on. The picture was taken by someone standing on the deck of the ship that had picked us up. I don't know who took the picture or how one of the uncles came to have it. In the picture, our boat looks like a toy boat floating in a big bowl of water. There are little people standing in the boat. We are among the people in the picture but I can't tell who is who because we are all so small. Small faces, small heads, small arms reaching out to touch small hands. Maybe the Americans on the ship were laughing at us. Maybe that's why it took them so long to lower the ladder. Maybe they laughed so hard at the sight of us so small, they started to roll around the deck like spilled marbles and they had to help one another to their feet and recall their own names—Emmett, Mike, Ron—and where they were from—Oakland, California; Youngstown, Ohio; Shinston, West Virginia—before they could let us climb up and say our names—Lan, Cuong, Hoang—and where we were from—Phan Thiet, Binh Thuan.

It didn't matter what I told them. The story could take place in the courtyard of our house in Vietnam or on the deck of the Navy ship that picked us up from the sea or in a hammock at the refugee camp in Singapore or in the belly of the airplane that carried us to California; it could take place in the heat of midday or in the cool of the evening or in the strange weather of one of my Ba's nightmares; it could smell of fish sauce or of hamburgers or of jasmine; it could be a description of a dream I had or a dog I saw or a boy I missed; it could be about the way my mother's hair smelled warm at night or the way the playground slide felt cold in the morning or the way the grass in the back garden tickled my ankles; it could be about how everything that happened to my Ba and the four uncles and me, happened "Suddenly," "Many years ago," and "Somewhere far away"—as in those fairy tales that the teacher read to the class every Friday.

The glass animals didn't blink. They didn't laugh. They never raised an eyebrow or tilted their heads as they listened. They didn't nod in agreement or stomp the ground to object. They didn't ask questions. They didn't seem to want to know anything. I got tired of talking to them and I sensed that if I kept them in the sun too long, they might shatter.

I would stretch the hem of my T-shirt out and lift the glass animals off the ledge, placing them one by one into the sail of my shirt. I could feel their skinny legs poking me through the cloth as I carried them back to the cabinet. I'd line the animals up tall, short, tall, just as Mel's mother had lined them up originally for Mel. I closed the glass doors of the display cabinet with the glass animals staring ahead. They didn't remember me. When I hid in the small space between the cabinet and the wall, they never turned their heads or pressed their faces against the glass doors of the cabinet to look for me. The uncles were unaware that it wasn't the butterfly but rather these glass animals that had no soul.

The butterfly sat in my shirt pocket, pressing against my body as I walked around Mel's office. I liked the weight of the butterfly. I liked it the way I liked standing in the back garden with my hands in my pockets and my eyes closed as I slowly turned my face toward the sun. The color of the butterfly when I held it up to the light was like the taste of the sun on those days when I stood in the back garden sticking my tongue out.

One Friday afternoon in December, a week before Christmas vacation, I tried to free the butterfly. The result was Mel told Ba, the four uncles and me to pack our things and get out. Ba said it wasn't my fault; it wasn't anybody's fault. Ba said these things happen.

On that day, I told the glass animals about a dream I'd had the night before. In it, I'd stolen one of the school crossing guards' signs and carried it back to Mel's house. I dragged the sign down the long hallway and stood it up like the mast of a ship. My Ba and the four uncles were asleep. I woke them and told them to climb onto the sign. I tied them to the signpost so they wouldn't fall off and as they waited for me, I ran from room to room, turning on all the faucets in the house.

I told the glass animals that the rushing water in the dream lifted my Ba, the four uncles and me out of the house, down the five steps, into the street, past the school and the uncles' pool hall, beyond the rows of identical apartment buildings, each with its rooms glowing white. As we sailed through the streets on our sign, I held the glass disk like a telescope up to my eye and through the body of my butterfly, I saw Ma standing on a faraway beach.

The glass animals listened patiently but had no opinions about my dream. I picked them up from the windowsill and carried them back to the display cabinet. I closed the cabinet and climbed onto Mel's leather swivel chair, twirling myself around and around. I spun myself dizzy trying to remember what Ma's face looked like in my dream and trying to think of a way to get my butterfly out of its glass disk.

When the chair stopped spinning, I noticed some broken glass on the bottom shelf of a bookcase near the display cabinet. I climbed down from the swivel chair and walked over to the bookcase. The butterfly was in my

T-shirt pocket; it pulled down my shirt as I crouched to study the broken glass.

It was a picture frame. The glass of the frame was shattered but the picture beneath it looked untouched. Smiling up through the broken glass was a young Mel and his young mother. They had their arms around each other in that sort of tight embrace that made me feel it was hard to breathe. But they seemed to like it. Their noses were pink and shiny. The old woman's teeth were bright then and incredibly even. Mel's curls glowed in the sun. Mel and his mother looked very well to me.

Like my Ba and me, Mel and his mother stood in a snowy place, leaning against a blue car. A shadow was thrown across the snow. It must have belonged to the person taking the picture.

My eyes glanced up at the pipe in the glass cabinet. It lay on its side, the bits of tobacco still stuffed in its bowl.

I stood up from the picture and looked around the room. The room felt crowded. Messy stacks of paper were crammed into the shelves. Half-empty boxes of books lay at odd angles on the floor, having been pushed one way and then another as Mel made his way around. Empty boxes stood on end.

My eyes scanned the four walls of Mel's office before settling on the space between the glass display cabinet and the wall near the door. I walked up to the space and measured it with my hands, pressing first one palm and then the other flat against the wall.

Keeping my eye on the space, I backed away from the wall until I was standing beside the desk at the center of the room. I took the disk from my shirt pocket and cupped it in one hand. I rocked it a little, feeling its weight in my palm.

The butterfly lay in the disk. It was motionless, like someone expert at holding his breath or playing dead.

I held the disk up to my ear and listened. My heart was beating and wouldn't be quiet. I held the disk at arm's length, shook my head, and then brought the disk back to my ear.

There, very faintly, was the sound. It was like a light, almost transparent, curtain rippling across a window.

I tightened my fingers around the glass disk, swung my arm as far back as it would go, and, aiming for the center of that small space—a space the width of three hands— I skipped once and swung my arm forward, letting the disk fly.

The disk flew hard and fast, but not where I had sent it. It crashed through the glass doors of the display cabinet. The animals' knees buckled. As they fell, some of the animals lost their heads while others' bodies broke in two. The broken bodies of some protected the bodies of others from shattering completely. Some lay on their sides, staring out the window.

The disk hit the back of the cabinet, bouncing off the china before shooting back out into the room. Mel's office filled with the sounds that animals make.

Ba and the uncles threw open the door.

I spun in the chair, my eyes scanning the ceiling for the butterfly.

"Shuh-shuh/shuh-shuh."

"Suh-top!/suh-top!"

"Shuh-shuh/shuh-shuh."

"Suh-top!"

palm

The trees in the neighborhood were palms and eucalyptus. Along the sides of many of the houses were bushes of white jasmine that bloomed in the evening. Young girls picked the flowers and, with a thread and needle, strung the blooms into garlands. They made themselves crowns and necklaces and bracelets. If allowed to, they would wear the flowers to bed. By morning, the garlands lay crushed and spent, the white having aged to yellow, but the fragrance remained across every throat and wrist and crown that had worn them.

During the day, the sun beat down hard on those streets, warping the sensations, muting the sight and sound and feel of everything. The chants of children skipping rope in the alley beneath an open window seemed to come from miles away. And the sound the rope made, as it brushed against the ground, was like that of a broom sweeping a courtyard—in another country. A couple fighting in an apartment across the way moved from room to room, from window to window, fighting the fight they would always be fighting, in which no one would ever be hurt. Nothing was urgent. You could pick up a ripe mango from the kitchen table and hold it to your nose. In the heat its scent would mingle with all the others: the sweat of children running; incense burning on the altar; clean clothes drying on the line; apples and oranges quartered and offered, without any fuss, to both the dead and the living.

In the shade of the evening, as you looked over the second-floor railing into the swimming pool below, the shapes of things that had happened would slowly take form and come into focus. The day would return to you, and with it, like a school of fish, all the other days. You could lean against the railing then and watch, with wonder, as the people, places, and objects from all the days gathered. In your mind's eye, they would glide and flicker, making their way across the darkening face of the swimming pool before, one by one, they would rise from the water and scale the air approaching where you stood leaning far over the rail, holding out your hand.

· · ·

The swimming pool was in the courtyard, beyond the rusted iron gates of the small red apartment building my father had found when Mel asked us to leave his place. One of the gates had hung lower than the other after my mother backed into it that summer, trying to park our family's new used Cadillac.

The night this happened, we had dragged our mattresses out of the bedroom and were lying on the living room floor, with the front door open to help break the summer heat. Other families in our building had done the same. I could hear voices all around. After a while, Ba fell asleep, but Ma and I lay awake, restless. She rolled out of bed and walked into the kitchen. I thought she was going to pour herself a glass of water. Instead, she took Ba's keys, which were hanging from a nail on the wall, and fishing her pocketbook out from under the mattress signaled for me to come with her.

Ma didn't know how to drive. We got into the car, and she threw her pocketbook on the dashboard. She put both hands on the steering wheel and rocked it back and forth.

"Let's see if this works," she said, slipping the key into the ignition. When the engine started, she smiled and patted the steering wheel. She practiced a couple of times, backing out and pulling into the parking space, and when she felt confident about those maneuvers, she backed the Cadillac into the middle of the street and turned on the lights. We sat there for a minute, giggling. She said, "This is easy. It's easier than riding a bicycle. We can't fall off!" She drove down the very middle of the street, gunning toward stop signs, taking wide left turns, bumping the windshield wipers on by accident so they swayed back and forth, making small squeaking sounds all the way around the block.

Like everyone else in the building, my father heard the crash. As he came running down the stairs, others came walking out of their apartments. Reassured to know that no one in their family was responsible for the present commotion, people leaned over the second-floor railing or ambled across the courtyard, gathering to see what had happened, and to whom.

My father fixed my mother with a look, but before he could say anything, she argued that it wasn't her fault. The car was as big as a boat, she said. Thank God the gates were there, or else the Cadillac would have shot straight into the pool. "And where," she asked, waving her hand toward the passenger seat, "would that have left the child and me?"

My father opened the driver's side door so my mother could step out of the car. I opened the passenger door myself and stepped out. Ma leaned back into the car and grabbed her pocketbook from the dashboard. She didn't have much money in it—she never would—but she liked carrying it everywhere she went. In one motion, she swung the pocketbook under her left arm, fixed it in place by pressing her left elbow tight against her side and reached for my hand. She calmly walked me up the sixteen steps back into our apartment.

Ba climbed into the Cadillac, gently backed it away from the mangled gates, turned the car off and remained sitting in the driver's seat, with the doors closed, the windows up and the lights off, thinking. He then drove the car to the house of a family friend; one of the four uncles Ba and I had come with to America and had lived with for two years, before Ma arrived. The uncle worked as a mechanic at a local garage and he was the one who convinced Ba to get Ma the used Cadillac, a "Welcome to America" present. Ba woke the uncle and, without any kind of explanation, told him that the car was too big. It was too much. He needed something else. The uncle sat up and reached for the pack of cigarettes he kept beside the bed. He thought it was a shame about the Cadillac, but said he understood. Ba gave the uncle the keys to the Cadillac and, a week later, the uncle brought by an orange Mercury Cougar. He said he knew it wasn't much smaller, but it was the best he could do. He threw the keys to Ba, and Ba hid them from Ma.

．　．　．

The morning after Ma crashed into the front gates, the landlord came by to check on the busted washing machine in the laundry room. As he approached, he saw the gates wide open, one of them dented and hanging by a hinge. Between them, the pool lay like a bright blue sheet. It rippled slightly but otherwise it was calm. When he reached the gates, he tried to close them. One gate swung forward easily but the broken one had to be picked up and walked into position. He felt uncomfortable doing this. It was like walking a drunk. But he did it anyway.

As the landlord half carried, half dragged the gate closed—inadvertently shutting himself out of his own courtyard—he silently cursed his tenants. He suspected each and every one of those living in the building's sixteen units. They were all capable of having done this. They were people who broke things: the washing machine, screen doors, kitchen sinks, windows, the back gate and now the front. And they let their children run wild.

Out of the corner of his eye, the landlord saw something flutter. It was an empty rice bag, hanging in an open window of the house next door. Years ago, that house, like many on the block, had begun as something pretty, with yellow curtains in the windows and flowering bushes out front. Had they been roses? It was so long ago. Now the house was nothing more than a shell. When a fire gutted the place, the owners never came to fix it or even to tear it down. The landlord noticed that the neighborhood children had taken over the house; tattered bits of cloth, like the empty rice bag, hung in the windows; the front yard, burnt dry by the sun, was littered with branches of eucalyptus and their cones, as if they'd been blown there by a summer storm.

On the other side of his apartment building was a Church of Jehovah's Witnesses. It was covered in beige stucco and, with its two small watchtowers, looked like a miniature castle on a cake. All it lacked, thought the landlord, were a couple of sentinels, one in each tower to keep guard over the neighborhood.

A baby cried. A woman's voice tried to console it, murmuring in a language the landlord didn't understand. These sounds came from somewhere up on his second floor.

The landlord looked at the gates to his apartment building. They were crookedly yet firmly in place, one leaning heavily against the other. He struggled with the gates for a moment before managing to push his way through.

On his way past the swimming pool, he bent down and picked up some leaves that had gathered in a corner. He cupped the leaves in his hand and felt the water drip between his fingers. Holding his hand away from his body so as not to drip water on himself, the landlord went to see about the washing machine.

I lived upstairs, in a one-bedroom apartment with my mother and my father. She worked as a seamstress, doing piecework at our kitchen table. He worked as a welder at a factory that made space heaters. Neither of them wanted to be doing it; Ma wanted to have a restaurant, and Ba wanted to have a garden. On weekends, my mother liked to watch kung fu movies at the Chinese movie theater on El Cajon Boulevard and my father liked to drink with his friends.

The three of us slept in one room. My parents' double bed was separated from my single bed by a side table with a lamp on it. The base of the lamp was a figurine of an old Chinese man crouching on a rock, his wide pant legs pushed up past his knees. In his hands he held a fishing pole, and his eyes were forever fixed on one spot in the pool of light that was cast back down on the table.

That was the summer when the older boys in the neighborhood started diving off the second-floor railing into the swimming pool in the courtyard below. From our front windows, we would see one boy after another stand poised on the railing for a minute, bend his knees, push off and disappear as the other boys, each waiting his turn, hooted their approval.

From where she sat working at the kitchen table, my mother had a clear view of the divers. "Someone is going to die trying to fly like that," she'd say, carefully feeding small pieces of fabric through her sewing machine. Her words were drowned out by the sewing machine's noise and the boys' cries of "Jump! Jump! Jump!" "Hurry up!" "C'mon!"

I didn't know how to swim then, so my mother told me never to go near the pool. That summer, as I sat with her while she worked, she would issue her warnings. About the pool she told me, " Look at you; you're as small as a mouse. The water is much deeper than you think." About cars she said, "They can hit you and keep going." About the needle on her sewing machine she said, "Watch your fingers; it can move much faster than you can run!" And about boys she warned, "They will try to press you into it."

I wasn't scared. I was curious. I wondered about the swimming pool. How deep was it at its deepest point? How many people would that be, if they stood stacked, each on the shoulders of the one before, with all those beneath holding their breath for how long? What did it feel like to jump as I'd watched the older boys do, leaping off the railing with a sudden push of their feet? Some of them made funny faces on their way down. Some ran in place, their arms and legs racing in the air. One boy, imitating Road Runner, bugged out his eyes and yelled, "Meep, meep!" Others closed their eyes and looked like they were sleeping. They pressed their arms fast against their sides, pointed their toes and plunged into the water like knives. As fast as they fell, the boys popped up again, laughing. Each boy's hair would be plastered against his forehead, every strand shining and neatly in place, as if he was headed for the first day of school or a church Communion or a meeting with a girl.

That summer, with my parents asleep in the bed next to mine, my father lying on his back, his breathing like a whistle, my mother lying on her side, one arm thrown across his chest and her long hair fanning out behind her, I'd lie awake and think about things.

With the sheet pushed down to my waist and one arm cushioning my head, I'd gaze at the rectangular shape of the window above my parents' bed and picture fish in the sea, their gills fluttering like eyelashes; clouds of sand roaming the desert for thousands and thousands of miles; the bright green streak of a gecko darting across a wall;

how it felt to ride a horse and whether it made any difference whether it was a black or a spotted one.

On weekends, my mother and I would walk to the Chinese movie theater on El Cajon Boulevard and watch the kung fu movies. We'd push through the glass revolving doors and I'd run across the red carpet to the little man with the slow eye who sat inside the ticket booth and buy two tickets for whatever was showing. The movies we watched were epics; the stories so long and involved, Ma said we could come back every weekend for the rest of our lives and still there would be more to tell.

In these movies, the warriors could fly. Dressed in robes with swords slung across their back and hair flowing to their feet, they would point their fingers or turn a wrist in elaborate ways and go gliding across rooftops or float straight up into the arms of trees. There wasn't much dialogue in these movies. The warriors didn't do much talking. Ma said it wasn't their nature. To express themselves, they would pick up swords or bamboo spikes and run at each other, screaming.

I had a hard time remembering who was fighting whom and which characters were related and which were the good and which the bad. As they fought, they would insult each other, and these insults would occasionally appear in English subtitles. To impress my mother, I read the titles out loud. "As long as I am on this earth with you," I would shout toward the screen, "I must seek to smash your head in! Ha-ha!" "Very good," Ma would say, smacking my knee with her fingertips.

After the movies, we'd walk across the street to the Vietnamese restaurant with the big smiling plastic cow's head on its roof. The restaurant's specialty was beef noodle soup. We'd order two bowls and while we waited for the food to arrive, I'd practice pointing my fingers and cupping my hands as I'd seen the kung fu warriors do.

"It's rude to point," my mother would say. "If you don't watch out, the muscles in your hands will lock into those odd positions and you'll never be able to hold your chopsticks properly."

She was full of warnings that summer. "If you dance with your shadow," she'd say, "you'll go crazy." "If you run around barefoot all summer, your feet will burn and fall off." "If you swallow fruit seeds, trees will grow inside of you until the branches come out of your ears."

She told me that my chicken pox scars were really diamonds and the day I met a boy who recognized this, I was to marry him. I told her that I didn't want to get married; what I wanted was to fly like the people in the movies. She said, "Listen to me. How many times have I told you? People look like they're flying but in fact they're being pulled along by invisible strings." I said that I didn't believe her and she said, "All right. Maybe those people"—and she would point across the street to the Chinese movie theater—"Maybe they were flying. But that was a long time ago." And she would draw out the words "long time ago" so that they sounded like three stones, one following another, down into a well.

The people from the Church of Jehovah's Witnesses next door would come and visit our building regularly. They arrived in pairs, a man and a woman, and handed out pamphlets with colorful drawings of the Heavenly Kingdom.

The first time they came to our apartment, my father opened the door and said, "We no God, we Buddha." The next time they came, he told me to answer the door. I opened the door and said, "We're Buddhists." But I knew this wasn't true; my mother is Catholic. She had a painting of Jesus on velvet, kneeling beside a boulder, praying to a starry purple sky, his lips bright red. The painting hung on the wall behind me and I wondered, as I stood there lying, if the Jehovah's Witnesses could see it.

My friends told me that if you gave the church people the chance, they would open their little books and pointing to the pictures of fresh fruit say things like "This is

Heaven" and "Here is the Kingdom of God where no one suffers," their fingers tracing an invisible line connecting all the healthy people walking through the sunlit fields.

My friends and I took the pamphlets the church people handed out and studied the drawings of people having picnics on the banks of a long blue river or harvesting wheat or standing arm in arm, looking into each other's eyes. To us, these pictures were more unbelievable than the warriors we saw flying in the kung fu movies. As far as we could understand it, the church on our street was like a ladder to the Kingdom.

When the Jehovah's Witnesses weren't there, we chased each other up and down the stairs and around the towers of their castle. That summer, we made up a game called Kingdom. At first, Kingdom was about pretending that we were in Heaven. We tried to be the people in the little books. We swept the stairs and kept the castle clean. We walked around smiling, waving to invisible people in our heavenly community. We put our hands on each other's shoulders and said things like "My son," "My friend," "God knows." When we got bored, Kingdom became about having fights and waging war.

We made up stories about ships at sea, on the lookout for pirate ships. We divided into warring groups and occupied separate towers. Each tower was a country. The leaders and the people of both countries yelled insults back and forth until someone took off a flip-flop and beat it against a tower wall, yelling, "Attack!" We threw eucalyptus cones and chased each other out into the street. We fought with sticks and branches, plunging the sticks like daggers and waving the branches like swords. We fell to our knees clutching our sides or hung our heads crying, "My eye! My eye!" We agreed the best way to die was to wiggle on the floor or stumble slowly step by step, twitching and trembling, down the stairs. We fought over which side had killed more people and because we usually couldn't agree, we'd have to collect more eucalyptus cones and have another war.

The youngest kids had a hard time dying. We had to explain to them that when they were out, they were out: they couldn't just open their eyes again and keep on fighting. They had to be reminded that they were dead. "But what should we do?" they'd ask. "Just wait over there," we'd yell, pointing to the two tall palm trees on the sidewalk in front of the church.

The ones who understood would stand like little ghosts between the tall trees and clap their hands together when their side was winning or wave their arms in the air when they thought their side was losing. They yelled: "Run!" "Get her!" "Come this way! No, THIS way!"

. . .

Though my parents didn't want me playing near the swimming pool, they both liked having the pool in the courtyard. My mother said it wasn't the sea but it was nice to open the door and have some water.

In the evenings, our family and other families in our building brought chairs out and sat on the terraces. The adults talked among themselves while the kids played ball in the courtyard or games of Marco Polo and Green Light–Red Light in the swimming pool. Leaning over the railing on the second floor, I'd watch my friends in the pool below, watch my parents walk around, talking with the neighbors. The adults talked about jobs and cars and what was on sale at the grocery store and how big the newborn baby had grown and whether the landlord would replace the broken washing machine or try to fix it again even though, as one woman reminded everyone, the last time he tried, it jumped up and down like an angry horse. In the pool, kids were tiptoeing up to each other only to freeze in mid-step. Holding strange contorted poses, they tried not to fall down laughing.

"Come down!" my friends would call up to me, waving their arms in the air. I'd look over to my mother, who shook her head no, and then to my father, who also shook his head no. "I can't," I'd yell down to my friends.

When the landlord pulled up in his truck to deliver the new washing machine, he caught the boys leaping off the second-floor railing into the swimming pool below. He ran over to the edge of the pool and shouted into the face of the boy who was climbing out, "Hey! Hey! Are you crazy?"

There were five boys waiting upstairs and they decided to jump together, landing with a big splash that enraged the landlord. "You're going to break your necks!" the landlord yelled.

The boys didn't care. They pulled themselves up and swung their bodies easily out of the water. They pulled their jeans on over their wet shorts and jumped on their bicycles and rode away, laughing. They didn't even bother to close the gates behind them.

Early one morning not long after that, a team of workmen pulled up to our building. They opened the crooked iron gates and started moving their equipment into the courtyard. They worked all day. First they roped off the area around the swimming pool. Then they drained all the water out of it. The water rolled across the courtyard and spilled onto the sidewalk before disappearing down the street. Once all the water had gone, the workmen began filling the empty pool with rocks. The rocks banged against the floor and the sides of the pool and rattled hard against each other.

When the pool was completely filled with rocks, the workmen poured cement over the rocks and drove away. In a couple of days, the first layer of cement had dried. The workmen returned and poured another. I don't remember how many layers of cement were poured into the pool before the workmen decided it was enough.

Like a strange sand-colored skin that had grown over the swimming pool, the cement took the pool's shape, even its curved edges. It hid from us nothing but the water.

When the workmen returned, they carried in a big wooden planter, and whatever was in the planter was covered with a black plastic bag. They placed the planter in the center of the courtyard, right in the middle of where the water used to be. When they cut away the plastic, what we saw was a squat baby palm tree.

One of the workmen gathered the plastic bag into his arms and rolled it into a bundle. He tossed the bundle into the back of the truck. Their work done, the men closed the gates behind them and drove away.

That night, my parents had an argument. My mother had just turned off the Chinese fisherman lamp. After a few minutes with the three of us lying in our beds, flat on our backs, staring at the ceiling, my mother asked my father why the landlord had done it.

"Done what?" my father asked. "You know what," my mother said. "He's the landlord. It's his building," my father said. My mother said, "It's ugly." "It doesn't matter," my father said. He turned toward the wall. My mother said, "It does matter. It's ugly. What is there to look at now?" My father didn't answer. My mother said, "I open the door and what is there to see?" "Well, what do you want to see?" my father asked. "Not a desert," my mother said.

Then no one said anything.

What was there to say?

I lay in bed and remembered the things I had seen in the swimming pool. I remembered the body of a boy, gliding along the floor of the pool, sunlight streaming across his bare back. I remembered the reflection of clouds, families of clouds, and birds, migrating. I remembered the leaves that floated to the edges of the swimming pool and nested there. I remembered how the glare of the sun made the water glint like a windowpane. I remembered the reflection of a ball bouncing in the courtyard and the clotheslines, strung from rail to rail, the sheets fluttering like banners in the air. But what I remembered most were the boys, flying. I remembered their bodies arcing through the air and plunging down. I remembered how their hands parted the water and how as they disappeared, the last thing I would see were the pale soles of their feet. Falling asleep, I remembered the brightness of the full moon, shimmering in the swimming pool, so close, so close, like a caught fish.

My friends and I fished out of the Dumpster the box in which the new washing machine had arrived and we dragged it to the backyard of the abandoned house next door. We laid the box on its side and pushed it against the trunk of a eucalyptus tree. We hung towels over the opening, fixing them in place with rocks. The box became part of our improvements to the house, like the convoy of grocery carts we'd pushed back from Safeway, arranging them, each upended, in a semicircle in the front yard as our lawn chairs.

We called the box The Other Room and then just, The Room. It was a small, dark place two people could crawl into together and sit, knee to knee.

Before any of us had come to the neighborhood, there had been a fire in this house and now the place was charred and crumbly. Most of the walls were black and you could walk through some of them. The rooms were small and crowded with burnt and broken things. There was no running water and no electricity in the house. Our parents didn't mind our playing there, so long as we washed our hands and feet before we went to bed at night. They called the house "The kids' house." "The kids are next door, in their house," we'd hear them tell one another.

Among the things we found when we first came into the house was an empty chest of drawers, a dusty mattress with broken springs, eight bent spoons, a dead lamp with a melted cord, ashy paper, two chairs with missing legs, one chair with a broken leg, smoke-stained curtains and scattered across the floor stuffing from the torn cushions of an orange plaid couch.

Also scattered across the floor were pictures of a couple. The woman had red hair and wore it piled high atop her head. The guy had short, spiky blond hair, skinny lips and very blue eyes. I didn't look at him too much. In the pictures, she has freckles and her skin is pale, almost shining. She doesn't look healthy although I imagine her skin was probably soft to the touch.

My favorite picture was the one in which the woman is sitting on the man's lap. He has one arm across her chest with the other reaching out toward where the camera would be. The man took the picture himself, holding the camera at arm's length. Neither of them is smiling exactly and she looks distracted, as if eager to get back to that cigarette she just lit and has been holding between two fingers of her left hand.

We dragged the dusty mattress out to the middle of the living room and took turns jumping on it. We pretended that the mattress was a trampoline with the potential to project us across oceans and into outer space if we jumped hard enough.

After playing on the trampoline, we'd pick through the empty kitchen cabinets and pretend to find french fries, hamburgers, and fried chicken, which we devoured loudly, with our mouths open. For dessert, we biked to the corner store across the street from our school. There, we would pool our pennies to buy a box of Lemon Heads or Atomic Red Hots, which we divided among ourselves as we stood in a circle. Sucking on our candies, we'd bike over to the school playground and there disbanded, running across the blacktop to climb the jungle gym, or hang by the backs of our knees from the monkey bars, or ride the swings standing up or bury each other up to our necks in the sandbox. As the sky darkened and we could smell the jasmine blooming, we would aim our bikes toward the Jehovah's Witnesses towers and ride home. Those of us who, like me, didn't have bikes would ride on someone else's handlebar. When we rode in a straight line, like the cars of a train, I'd be in front, the horn and the smoke announcing our arrival.

That summer, I went into The Room with a boy. After a few minutes of not saying anything, hardly even breathing, he put his hand on my chest. I said, "Hey." I thought my voice would come out high like an alarm but it came out low and quiet, with a lot of space around it. I felt the heat from his palm pass through my shirt. He moved his hand slowly across my chest and down. "Hey," I said. There it was again, not the alarm but the quiet. He stopped, his hand resting against my stomach. Neither of us moved. I touched my fingers to his wrist and then his forearm. Goose bumps formed beneath my fingertips. The boy shifted a little. I heard someone walking by outside. The footsteps came toward us and then went away. The boy slipped his other hand around my waist. I closed my eyes and followed the goose bumps up his arm, my fingers slipping under his shirtsleeve to rest on his shoulder. He leaned closer, his hand on my back now, his fingers pressing softly into me. Someone's mother called her name. It wasn't mine, but I opened my eyes anyway and backed out of the box.

I grabbed my sandals from the ground and swinging them in my hands, ran home. I threw the screen door open and let it slam shut behind me. Ma looked up from her sewing and, seeing that my feet were bare, told me to go wash them.

Lying in bed that night, I thought about the boy. I remembered the feeling of his shoulder in my hand, the roundness of it pressing against my palm. I brought two fingers to my throat and imagined they were lips—mine and then his—feeling for a pulse.

That was the summer I came out of the bathroom at the Chinese movie theater and saw my mother in the lobby talking to a man I'd never seen before. He was staring at her and she was staring at him as if they knew each other but didn't believe what they were seeing. My mother kept smiling and tucking her hair behind her ears. She had just gotten a haircut so actually her hair was already behind her ears.

I went over and stood next to her. The man noticed before my mother did and he smiled, but I didn't smile back. My mother told me to go wash my hands. I kept my eyes on the man and said, "I already washed my hands." She said, "Wash them again." I went into the bathroom and watched my mother and the man from behind the bathroom door. My mother and the stranger kept talking and smiling and then all of a sudden it was as though they were both backing away, each turning from the other, at the same time. Like a knot coming loose. He turned and walked toward the glass doors of the theater and she turned and walked toward the women's bathroom.

In the bathroom, my mother stood before the mirror and slowly wet her hands. She ran her fingers through her hair before pressing the backs of them to her cheeks and then her throat. As she fished around in her pocketbook, rearranging the contents, I watched her and thought that she didn't look like my mother. When she saw me staring at her, she said, "That was a friend from home. From when I was a girl." "Oh," I said, nodding, as if I understood. She looked at herself in the mirror and added, "From when I was a young girl." "Young like me?" I asked. She glanced at me and after a second of not saying anything, she shook her head and smiled. "No," she said, "a little older."

I was in the kissing box with the boy when someone beat against the box with a branch. "Hey, get out! It's our turn. You better not be making babies in there." I heard pebbles thrown against the cardboard. I let go of the boy's hand and felt his body turning in the dark. He kicked open the flaps of the box and the sun came in. When I leaned forward to step out, I felt the sun warming my knees, my wrist, the side of my arm and my face. I touched one bare foot to the ground and the ground was all heat and powdery dust.

One night I woke to the sound of my mother laughing in the bed across from mine. She was trying to take off my father's shoes but his legs were bent funny so she had to pull hard. The shape of my mother in the dark kept changing. She leaned back and I saw her hair slip loose from the bun on top of her head. Her hair fell down her neck, brushed her shoulders and fanned across her back.

My dad was drunk. He said, "I'm so tired. Come here. Forget about the shoes." He swung his arms in the air. He was drawing crooked hoops for her to step through. She stood up on the bed and walked toward him slowly. She was taller than everything now, but the bedsprings made her steps unsteady. She pressed her palm against the wall to balance herself. Standing over him she placed her foot on his chest. He wrapped his fingers around her ankle and said, "Come here. You're so far away." She shook her head and said, "You're ridiculous. Don't even know how to take your own shoes off." She put a hand on one hip and laughed at him. He stroked the calf of her leg and said, "Lie down here," patting his chest with his other hand. "Here," he said, patting his chest again, this time in a different place. My mother merely looked down at him. He caught her hand and pulled her to him.

I heard muffled laughter, whispers, the word "Anh" and then quiet.

Beside me my parents became long and dark bodies rising and falling like waves.

At night I watched as the shape of my hand kept changing in the dark. Here are five fingers. I made a fist. I made the mouth of a hungry bird. I made scissors. I held my hand in front of me. It was a page, a picture. I pulled it away, turned it around, and brought it back. It became another page, another picture. It was a door. I opened and closed it. There was a creaky hinge. I licked the side of my little finger and everything was quiet again. Two fingers in the air were feet running uphill. My hand curving backward was a dive into deep water.

There was a road my father took that summer which curved above a canyon of eucalyptus trees. It was a back road between an uncle's house and ours. The uncle must have been doing well that summer because it seemed like every other Sunday he would throw a party.

A party meant the women in the kitchen talking and cooking, the kids outside playing and the men in the living room drinking. When it got dark out, the kids were called inside to help with the dishes and then told to sit around and be quiet while the men finished their drinks. Tired and bored, we'd fight and then fall asleep in the hallway. When the men had drunk enough to feel happy, some even happy enough to cry, it was time to go home. As my father drove us home, the Mercury Cougar lurched at each curve in the road, as if it wanted to leap toward the stands of eucalyptus in the canyon below.

. . .

When the boy moved his hand across my chest, I saw my father's car sliding down the soft wall of the canyon. I stopped the boy's hand. "Hey . . ." There it was again; not the alarm but the quiet. I touched his forearm and then his wrist. I didn't know what to do next, so I closed my eyes.

The boy shifted a little and without thinking, I brought his hand up to my throat and then to my face. Guiding his fingers across my lips and against my cheek, I imagined that he was blind and learning, with his hand, what a face was. Here are lips, a nose, the bridge of a nose, I imagined explaining to him. Here are two closed eyelids, the tickle of eyelashes, the bones in the cheeks, the shape of the forehead, two brows. I raised his hand until his fingertips were brushing my eyebrows, and then I leaned forward and pressed my lips against his palm. He made a little sound, like "ah."

His palm felt warm and the sweat smelled sweet.

I stood at the window and looked down to where the swimming pool had been. Ma was working behind me, at the kitchen table. "Where does water go when it goes away?" I asked her. "It goes into the air or it goes into the ground," Ma said. I pictured a coin from her pocketbook being tossed into the air.

Down below, the palm looked lonely as an island. "What if someone goes down into water," I asked, "and doesn't come up?" "Don't know," my mother said. "Hand me that spool of thread."

My palms in the dark: the fingers of my left hand feeling for the lines on my right palm; the fingers of my right hand reaching for the lines on my left palm; back and forth in the dark. It takes me such a long time to trace a single line in the dark that the line seems to get longer and deeper, becoming a river, a tunnel, a trench or the roots of the trees my mother says are growing inside of me. If it's a tree, there aren't any leaves or fruit yet, just a trunk with the skinniest branches. If it's a trench, there aren't any people hiding in it yet. It's freshly dug and empty. If it's a tunnel, I'm not sure where it's leading. And if it's a river, I don't know which way it would be to the ocean. This line, falling off the side of my palm? Or this line, leading straight back into me? Sometimes I can't feel a single line on my hand and that's when I imagine that my palms are all sand, desert; no river, no tunnel, no trench, no tree; nothing between the sand and the sky but the smoothest open space.

It was into this open space that I imagined someone might fall. All that summer, while lying awake at night or leaning over the railing during the day, I'd close my eyes and with my arms out, palms up, I'd whisper, "Come here, come here, come here."

. . .

When the carnival came to our neighborhood and set up on the edge of the school playground, my friends and I went on a roller-coaster ride called the Super-Loop. Unlike other roller-coaster rides, this ride didn't go anywhere except in one big circle. You swooped into the air and curved down toward the ground, over and over, faster and faster, until everyone was screaming. When all the cars were at the top, with everyone hanging upside down, they'd stop the ride. Hanging like that, you couldn't help but notice all the people on the ground and how small they looked. You could see them standing and walking around down there but it was strange; the ground they were on didn't look like the ground you could stand on; it looked like a picture of the ground. From that height, it felt like there was nothing above you and there was nothing below you, as though the whole world were a roller coaster stopped at the peak with only a picture of a floating ground somewhere far below. You could lift up a corner of that ground and there would be nothing beneath it. Except maybe water.

There were so many days that summer when my parents would start off trying to have fun and end up tearing the house apart. I noticed that neither of them cried much during that time; he liked to sing when he was drunk, and when she was mad, she liked to scream and throw things. When they fought, I couldn't understand much of what they said. They'd jump around the house like two firecrackers.

I blamed everything on the summer; the heat, the lack of rain, the pool's having gone. There was nothing to keep them from fighting about everything or anything. For instance, burnt food.

My father came home late from work, drunk. For that reason, my mother didn't want to be kissed by him. But then later, in the dark, she got mad at him for being too drunk to kiss her. "Where's your mouth?" he asked. "That's my shoulder," she said. "Where's your mouth?" "That's my forehead. That's my other shoulder." "Where's your mouth?" "Just go to sleep!" she said, turning away from him.

The next morning, she wouldn't get out of bed to make him breakfast, and in the evening, she burned the dinner. When he asked, "What's this about?" she pointed to her lips and said, "This is my mouth. Are you blind? Here is my mouth. Not here," she said, slapping her shoulders, "or here," pointing to the side of her head.

Then they got into a big fight about nothing.

As they were moving from room to room, yelling and breaking things, I'd lock myself in the bathroom, fill the tub with water, strip down to my underwear, climb in and pretend I was at the ocean on the world's hottest day. At the ocean, with my body covered completely in salt water,

I could listen to them and then not listen to them. I could move my body down so the waves cupped my ears and then move my body up, my head rising out of salt water to catch her saying, "You used to," and then down into the water again, nothing but waves crashing and then up again to hear him say, "Tired" or "What can I," and then as I dipped my head down, I'd hear her cut him off, "Forget it," she'd say. And when the awful quiet came, I'd break it by filling the tub with more and more water.

After fighting with each other, my parents would make up with me. Ma would walk to the market with her pocketbook under her arm and bring home a bag of sweet oranges or sticks of sugarcane. Ba would pull a piece of rock candy out of his pocket and break it into crystals on the kitchen counter. They'd both say, "Look what I found for you." As if they had dug it up or it had dropped from the sky and all they had to do was catch it and carry it home to me.

When Ma first arrived in America, she had very long hair. It didn't flow to her feet but it was thick and straight and black and you could grab it by the fistful and hold it to your face. After she cut it that summer, she looked more like the women who read the news on TV. "Modern" was how she described it. She didn't want to be a seamstress anymore, working all day long, her foot pumping the pedal so the machine would spin and murmur and the needle would go jab-a-dab-dab at her fingertips.

Ma worked at the kitchen table, surrounded by bags filled with the houses, clouds, suns, trees, and flowers that she'd sewn. These bags were picked up at the end of every week and taken to a factory where they would be sewn on baby blankets.

Ma cleared the kitchen table and showed me how the shapes that she'd been working on that summer would be arranged on those baby blankets she had never seen. Like a picture a child had drawn with crayons, the blanket would have a small white house with two windows, one door, and a pointed brown roof. The house sat on a patch of green grass, next to a tall tree. There were fat, doughy clouds above the house and a sun the yellow of lemons. Red and orange flowers grew to either side of the house.

Each part of the picture had a colorful face and a blank back. My mother sewed the front and the back together, making sure to leave a small opening so she could fill their insides with bunches of cotton wooling. When the pictures puffed out, she sewed them shut. My mother worked very fast, turning things out like a factory. I imagined that the sharp little needle was the loudmouthed man on a factory floor, shouting out orders for her to go faster. Faster than yesterday! Faster toward tomorrow!

. . .

The factory where my father worked as a welder specialized in a certain kind of space heater. The kind that looked like a skinny white leg that glowed red when you turned it on. My mother thought it was unfortunate that the heaters were so skinny. She said, "A skinny heater's like a skinny person. How can it keep you warm?" Ba explained that though the heater was thin, it was designed to be efficient: you could stand it in the corner and the heat would radiate out from "that little leg," and warm the whole room. Ma found this hard to believe and worried that the company my father worked for would go out of business for making such skinny heaters. Sometimes my parents would fight about it. Ma thought Ba should say something, but Ba said there was nothing he could do about it and, besides, he would have rather been a gardener.

That summer, he'd stand in the doorway of our apartment and stare at the concrete courtyard. "It may be time to move," he'd say. Shaking his head, he'd tell my mother and me that when they drained the pool, they should have filled it with soil. He could have grown us a jungle in the courtyard. "If that had happened," he told me, "you and your friends could have been the wild animals, charging through the jungle two by two."

I was lying in one tower of the Jehovah's Witnesses castle and my friend was lying in the other. I pulled the bottom of my T-shirt up to my chin and ran a hand across the two lumps on my chest. They felt paltry. Each was barely the size of a spoonful of rice. Unless I pinched them, I couldn't feel anything. Sometimes the fabric of my T-shirt rubbing against the tip of them tickled me. "Tickles," I yelled over to my friend. "That's all?" she yelled back, indignant. I heard her stand up in her tower and groan. As she came running down her stairs and over to my tower, I pictured her skinny ankles and her white sandal straps. At the top of my stairs, she announced, "They hurt me all the time." I shrugged my shoulders. "What can I do?" I said. "You'll see," she promised. "Someday you're going to suffer too."

She was standing above me now. Behind her head I could see the two tall palm trees in front of the church and beyond the palm trees, the sky, pale blue with a few clouds. The heat of the tiles against my back made me sleepy. The tower was full of eucalyptus cones since we had played war earlier that day. I reached over and picked up a cone and bit into it. It tasted bitter. I threw it into the air and heard it land and roll along the sidewalk. "I feel like taking my shirt off," I told her. "Why don't you?" she said. "It's not like you have anything to hide."

I took off my shirt and bunched it into a pillow to rest my head against. My friend sat down behind me, crossing her legs under herself, like my father's wooden statue of the Buddha. She leaned back against the wall, tapping her fingers against her bare knees.

I closed my eyes and imagined how, if I had my way, I'd run around with my shirt off all the time and spend my days climbing trees and my nights sleeping in one of these towers. While I slept, the sky would be dark as the back of a woman's long head of hair and all the stars would be the small white flowers she was wearing in it. Throughout the night, the eucalyptus trees would drop their cones, trying to wake me, and from inside the tops of the palms I would hear the rustling of small brown birds, the color of dust, nestled close together, slowly turning in their sleep.

I was almost asleep when I felt my friend's hands in my hair. She lowered her face toward mine. "Hey, boy," she said. "Upside down, you look like a boy. You look like the brother of . . ." And she said my name.

I looked at the sky. Looked at the clouds. I wanted to go to sleep. I closed my eyes. I could still feel my friend's fingers in my hair. I heard her ask, "Is it true that you had a—" "No," I said, pushing her hands away and sitting up. She touched my bare back and I pulled away. "Don't," I said, reaching for my shirt.

One Sunday, late in the summer, my parents decided to throw a party. When I asked if there was anything I could do to help, Ma told me to run to the corner store and buy her another bag of ice. As I was putting on my sandals, she opened her pocketbook, took out a dollar bill and handed it to me. "Hurry," she said.

· · ·

I walked the three long blocks down Orange to Euclid. The liquor store was on the corner. The screen door was closed and the store looked dark. I stepped into the cool and quiet inside. There was a tall man with thick hair standing behind the counter. He had a newspaper spread open across the counter and was leaning over it, reading. As I walked by him, he looked up and said, "Hi, there." I turned my head toward him and said, "Hi, there," in the same tone of voice. Then I laughed to myself, thinking, You bird. You parrot. You Polly. I mouthed the words Polly, Polly, Polly, as I walked between the tall shelves of bottles, making my way slowly toward the freezers at the back of the store.

I walked past the bottles of golden whiskey, past the bottles of vodka clear as water or rubbing alcohol, and stopped at the cognac bottles. Each bottle had a red wax seal on it, the kind of seal that gets stamped on letters delivered by horseback to people in castles. I raised my finger to the bottle and traced the *C* that was pressed into the seal. It left a light streak of dust on my fingertip but the *C* came up brighter, like a red ring I could slip my finger into.

I opened the tall freezer door, grabbed a bag of ice and carried it in my arms to the front of the store. The man had put away his newspaper and was now standing with his arms folded across his chest. I smiled at him and dropped the bag of ice on the counter.

Next to the cash register were plastic containers of beef jerky and a display rack of sunglasses. The rack creaked when I spun it and the man said, "Makes a racket." With the change from the ice, I bought a box of Lemon Heads. The man offered me a paper bag for the ice but I didn't take it. I wanted to carry the ice home in my arms, because it was still warm out. I put the box of candy in my pocket, wrapped my arms around the bag of ice and said, "Bye," to the man. As I walked through the screen door, I heard him say, "Bye, now," in my tone of voice.

I stood on the street corner, next to a bum who was eating a mango that smelled really good. He'd already pushed the button. We waited for the light to change. The open red hand flashed and then the white walking body, and then the sound like a mechanical bird. As I ran across the street, I heard the box of candy rattle in my pocket and I felt the coolness of the ice against my chest and throat.

When I got to the other side of the street, I looked back and saw that the bum hadn't moved. "C'mon!" I yelled. He shook his head. He was staying right there. He pushed the button and kept waiting.

I started walking home.

As I walked, I could see the Jehovah's Witnesses castle up the street. I thought I saw the shape of someone standing in the far tower. The sky was bright, blue, and cloudless. The sun warmed the top of my head and my arms. I saw the towers and the sky. I saw the dried-out lawns of my neighborhood. I saw some kid's name scratched into the sidewalk. RAMONE 1980. Two palm prints lay beside his name. They were pressed deep into the cement. I pictured a boy kicking his shoes off and doing a handstand, the sun reflecting off the soles of his bare feet. There was some glass scattered across the road, and where the sunlight hit the glass, I saw how it made the road sparkle like a long black river.

What happened next was just a feeling. Like heat or hunger or dizziness or loneliness or longing. My brother, making no sounds and casting no shadow, was walking behind me. There, again, was the familiar feeling of warmth, of his body beside my body. I could lean back, I could close my eyes and fall down a flight of stairs or off the second-floor railing, and he would be there to catch me; I was certain of it. I needed only turn around and there would be his face, his hands.

I could throw my arms around his neck and then, pushing him away, holding him at arm's length, I could ask him all my questions: Where did you go? Why didn't you take me with you? Was it cold there?

I had been waiting for him but something kept me from going to him.

· · ·

Very slowly, as if I had been riding a bicycle underwater and was now trying to make it turn, I heard myself say,

I can't.

I can't.

I can't. Ma's waiting for me and I'm going back to school in two weeks and—

I can't.

The bag of ice slipped in my arms. I leaned down to catch it and as I pulled it closer to me, I thought I felt my brother's breath upon me. This was not the warmth I'd felt earlier, but a chill now at the center of my spine. The feeling was so confusing and frightening, I ran.

I ran past the towers and saw no one. I ran through the broken gates, across the courtyard, where the swimming pool had been, my arm brushing against the small baby palm. Somehow my legs carried me up the sixteen steps and I burst, breathless, into our apartment.

"What happened?" my mother asked, walking out of the kitchen. "My brother—" I said. "He was . . . my brother." Shivering, I said, "He wanted me to go . . . and I wanted to but—"

. . .

Ma leaned down and put her hands on my shoulders. Her hands were wet. She pressed down hard on my shoulders, "Stop! Stop!" she said, shaking me. I clutched the bag of ice and told myself I would never let go of it. I said, "He was—" And she said, "Stop it." And I said, "My brother—" And she said, "Stop!"

I stopped and everything went quiet. So quiet, I couldn't hear a sound. I thought I wasn't breathing anymore. I looked around me. The apartment was filled with adults, all leaning toward me with their big eyes and furrowed brows. My friends were standing outside, looking in through the screen door and the windows. "What is it?" That was my father's voice, floating over to me. He lifted the bag of ice from my arms and I noticed that my shirt was wet. It stuck to me. I saw the slight outline of my breasts and now thought of two fists full of sand.

"I flew here." That was my voice. "I flew here." That was my voice again. Someone laughed. The sound was like a ball, bouncing once and then slowly rolling away. There was a pebble in my sandal. When I took a step forward to run after the sound of the rolling ball, the pebble slipped to the sole of my foot and I stepped on it. Startled, I put my arms out to steady myself and that's when I noticed my hands.

I held my hands out in front of me. I turned them back and forth and didn't recognize them. The fingertips were wrinkled with cold, as if I'd been swimming for hours.

I stood absolutely still. Someone called my name and I didn't answer. Someone touched me and I raised my hands to my face.

I stood in that small room and wept into the desert of my palms.

the gangster we are all looking for

Vietnam is a black-and-white photograph of my grandparents sitting in bamboo chairs in their front courtyard. They are sitting tall and proud, surrounded by chickens and a rooster. Between their feet and the dirt of the courtyard are thin sandals. My grandfather's broad forehead is shining. So too are my grandmother's famous sad eyes. The animals are oblivious, pecking at the ground. This looks like a wedding portrait though it is actually a photograph my grandparents had taken late in life, for their children, especially for my mother. When I think of this portrait of my grandparents in their last years, I always envision a beginning. To or toward what, I don't know, but always a beginning.

.   .   .

When my mother, a Catholic schoolgirl from the South, decided to marry my father, a Buddhist gangster from the North, her parents disowned her. This is in the photograph, though it is not visible to the eye. If it were, it would be a deep impression across the soft dirt of my grandparents' courtyard. Her father chased her out of the house, beating her with the same broom she had used every day of her life, from the time she could stand up and sweep until that very morning that she was chased away.

The year my mother met my father, there were several young men working at her parents' house, running errands for her father, pickling vegetables with her mother. It was understood by everyone that these men were courting my mother. My mother claims she had no such understanding.

She treated these men as brothers, sometimes as uncles even, later exclaiming in self-defense: I didn't even know about love then!

Ma says love came to her in a dark movie theater. She doesn't remember what movie it was or why she'd gone to see it, only that she'd gone alone and found herself sitting beside him. In the dark, she couldn't make out his face but noticed that his profile was handsome. She wondered if he knew she was watching him out of the corner of her eye.

Watching him without embarrassment or shame. Watching him with a strange curiosity, a feeling that made her want to trace and retrace his silhouette with her fingertips until she'd memorized every feature and could call his face to mind in any dark place she passed through. Later, in the shadow of the beached fishing boats on the blackest nights of the year, she would call him to mind, his face a warm companion for her body on the edge of the sea.

In the early days of my parents' courtship, my mother told stories. She confessed elaborate dreams about the end of war: foods she'd eat (a banquet table, mangoes piled to the ceiling); songs she'd make up and sing, clapping her hands over her head and throwing her hair like a horse's mane; dances she'd dance, hopping from one foot to the other. Unlike the responsible favorite daughter or sister she was to her family, with my father, in the forest, my mother became reckless, drunk on her youth and the possibilities of love. Ignoring the chores to be done at home, she rolled her pants up to her knees, stuck her bare feet in puddles, and learned to smoke a cigarette.

She tied a vermilion ribbon in her hair. She became moody. She did her chores as though they were favors to her family, forgetting that she ate the same rice, was dependent on the same supply of food. It seemed to her the face that now stared back at her from deep inside the family well was the face of a woman she had never seen before. At night she lay in bed and thought of his hands, the way his thumb flicked down on the lighter and brought fire to her cigarette. She began to wonder what the forests were like before the American planes had come, flying low, raining something onto the trees that left them bare and dying. She remembered her father had once described to her the smiling broadness of leaves, jungles thick in the tangle of rich soil.

One evening, she followed my father in circles through the forest, supposedly in search of the clearing that would take them to his aunt's house. They wandered in darkness, never finding the clearing much less the aunt she knew he never had.

"You're not from here," she said.

"I know."

"So tell me, what's your aunt's name?"

"Xuan."

"Spring?"

"Yes."

She laughed. I can't be here, she thought.

"My father will be looking for me—"

"It's not too late. I'll walk you home."

In the dark, she could feel his hand extending toward her, filling the space between them. They had not touched once the entire evening and now he stood offering his hand to her. She stared at him for a long time. There was a small scar on his chin, curved like her fingernail. It was too dark to see this. She realized she had memorized his face.

My first memory of my father's face is framed by the coiling barbed wire of a military camp in South Vietnam. My mother's voice crosses through the wire. She is whispering his name and with this utterance, caressing him. Over and over, she calls him to her, "Anh Minh, Anh Minh." His name becomes a tree she presses her body against. The calling blows around them like a warm breeze and when she utters her own name, it is the second half of a verse that begins with his. She drops her name like a pebble into a well. She wants to be engulfed by him, "Anh Minh, em My. Anh Minh, em My."

The barbed wire gates open and she crosses through to him. She arrives warm, the slightest film of sweat on her bare arms. To his disbelieving eyes she says, "It's me, it's me." Shy and formal and breathless, my parents are always meeting for the first time, savoring the sound of a name, marveling at the bones of the face cupped by the bones of the hand.

I trail behind them, the tip of their dragon's tail. I am drawn along, like a silken banner on the body of a kite.

. . .

For a handful of pebbles and my father's sharp profile, my mother left home and never truly returned. Picture a handful of pebbles. Imagine the casual way he tossed them at her as she was walking home from school with her girlfriends. He did this because he liked her. Boys are dumb that way, my mother told me. A handful of pebbles, to be thrown in anger, in desperation, in joy. My father threw them in love. Ma says they touched her like warm kisses, these pebbles he had been holding in the sun. Warm kisses on the curve of her back, sliding down the crook of her arm, grazing her ankles and landing around her feet in the hot sand.

What my father told her could have been a story. There was no one in the South to confirm the details of his life. He said he came from a semi-aristocratic northern family. Unlacing his boot, he pulled out his foot and directed her close attention to how his second toe was significantly longer than the others. "A sure sign of aristocracy," he claimed. His nose was high, he said, because his mother was French, one of the many mistresses his father had kept. He found this out when he was sixteen. That year, he ran away from home and came south.

"There are thieves, gamblers, drunks I've met who remind me of people in my family. It's the way they're dreamers. My family's a garden full of dreamers lying on their backs, staring at the sky, drunk and choking on their dreams." He said this while leaning against a tree, his arms folded across his bare chest, his eyes staring at the ground, his shoulders golden.

She asked her mother, "What does it mean if your second toe is longer than your other toes?"

"It means . . . your mother will die before your father," her mother said.

"I heard somewhere it's a sign of aristocracy."

"Huh!"

When my mother looked at my father's bare feet she saw ten fishing boats, two groups of five. Within each group, the second boat ventured ahead, leading the others. She would climb a tree, stand gripping the branch with her own toes and stare down at his. She directed him to stand in the mud. There, she imagined what she saw to be ten small boats surrounded by black water, a fleet of junks journeying in the dark.

She would lean back and enjoy this vision, never explaining to him what it was she saw. She left him to wonder about her senses as he stood, cigarette in hand, staring at her trembling ankles, and not moving until she told him to.

I was born in the alley behind my grandparents' house. At three in the morning, my mother dragged herself out of the bed in the smaller house where she and my father lived after they married. My father was away, fighting in the war. Ma's youngest sister had come to live with her, helping her with my older brother, who was just a baby then. Ma left the two of them sleeping in the hammock, my brother lying in the crook of my aunt's arm, and set out alone.

She cut a crooked line on the beach. Moving in jerky steps, like a ball tossed on the waves, she seemed to be bounced along without direction. She walked to the schoolhouse and sat on the ground before it, leaning against the first step. She felt grains of sand pressing against her back. Each grain was a minute pinprick, and the pain grew and grew. Soon she felt as though her back would erupt, awash in blood. She thought, I am going to bleed to death. She put her hands on her belly. We are going to die.

In front of the schoolhouse lay a long metal tube. No one knew where it came from. It seemed to have been there always. Children hid inside it, crawled through it, spoke to each other from either ends of it, marched across it, sat upon it and confided secrets beside it. There had been so little to play with during the school recess. This long metal tube became everything. A tarp was suspended over it, to shield it from the sun. The tube looked like a blackened log in a room without walls. When the children sat in a line on the tube, their heads bobbing this way and that in conversation, it seemed they were sitting on a canopied raft.

The night I was born, my mother, looking at the tube, imagined it to be the badly burnt arm of a dying giant buried in the sand. She could not decide whether he had been buried and was trying to get out or whether he had tried to bury himself in the sand but had failed to cover his arm in time. In time for what? She had heard a story about a girl in a neighboring town who was killed during a napalm bombing. The bombing happened on an especially hot night, when this girl had walked to the beach to cool her feet in the water. They found her floating on the sea. The phosphorus from the napalm made her body glow, like a lantern. In her mind, my mother built a canopy for this girl. She started to cry, thinking of the buried giant, the floating girl, these bodies stopped in mid-stride, on their way somewhere.

She began to walk toward the tube. She had a sudden urge to be inside it. The world felt dangerous to her and she was alone. At the mouth of the tube, she bent down, her belly blocking the mouth. She tried the other side, the other mouth. Again, her belly stopped her. "But I remember," she muttered out loud, "as a girl I sometimes slept in here." This was what she wanted now, to sleep inside the tube.

"Tall noses come from somewhere—"
"Not from here."
"Not tall noses."

．．．

Eyes insinuate, moving from her nose to mine then back again. Mouths suck in air, color it into the darkest shade of contempt, then spit it at her feet as she walks by. I am riding on her hip. I am the new branch that makes the tree bend but she walks with her head held high. She knows where she pulled me from. No blue eye.

Ma says war is a bird with a broken wing flying over the countryside, trailing blood and burying crops in sorrow. If something grows in spite of this, it is both a curse and a miracle. When I was born, she cried to know that it was war I was breathing in, and she could never shake it out of me. Ma says war makes it dangerous to breathe, though she knows you die if you don't. She says she could have thrown me against the wall, until I broke or coughed up this war that is killing us all. She could have stomped on it in the dark, and danced on it like a madwoman dancing on gravestones. She could have ground it down to powder and spat on it, but didn't I know? War has no beginning and no end. It crosses oceans like a splintered boat filled with people singing a sad song.

Every morning Anh wakes up in the house next to mine, a yellow duplex she and I call a town house since we found out from a real estate ad that a town house is a house with an upstairs and a downstairs. My father calls Anh "the chicken egg girl." Early each morning Anh's mother loads a small pushcart with stacks of eggs and Anh walks all over Linda Vista selling eggs before school. Her backyard is full of chickens and one rooster. Sometimes you can see the rooster fly up and balance himself on the back gate. From his perch, he'll crow and crow, on and off, all day long, until dark comes.

We live in the country of California, the province of San Diego, the village of Linda Vista. We live in old Navy Housing bungalows built in the 1940s. Since the 1980s, these bungalows house Vietnamese, Cambodian, and Laotian refugees from the Vietnam War. When we moved in, we had to sign a form promising not to put fish bones in the garbage disposal.

We live in a yellow house on Westinghouse Street. Our house is one story, made of wood and plaster. Between our house and another one-story house are six two-story houses. Facing our row of houses, across a field of brown dirt, sits another row of yellow houses, same as ours, watching us like a sad twin. Linda Vista is full of houses like ours, painted in peeling shades of olive green, baby blue, and sun-baked yellow.

There's new Navy Housing on Linda Vista Road, the long street that takes you out of here. We see the Navy people watering their lawns, their children riding pink tricycles up and down the culs-de-sac. We see them in Victory Supermarket, buying groceries with cash. In Kelley Park they have picnics and shoot each other with water guns. At school their kids are Most Popular, Most Beautiful, Most Likely to Succeed. Though there are more Vietnamese, Cambodian, and Laotian kids at the school, in the yearbook we are not the most of anything. They call us Yang because one year a bunch of Laotian kids with the last name Yang came to our school. The Navy Housing kids started calling all the refugee kids "Yang."

Yang. Yang. Yang.

Ma says living next to Anh's family reminds her of Vietnam because the blue tarp suspended above Anh's backyard is the bright blue of the South China Sea. Ma says, isn't it funny how sky and sea follow you from place to place as if they too were traveling.

Thinking of my older brother, who was still in Vietnam, I ask Ma, "If the sky and the sea can follow us here, why can't people?"

Ma ignores my question and says even Anh reminds her of Vietnam, the way she sets out for market each morning.

Ba becomes a gardener. Overnight. He buys a truck full of equipment and a box of business cards from Uncle Twelve, who is moving to Texas to become a fisherman. The business cards read "Tom's Professional Gardening

Service" and have a small green picture embossed on them, a man pushing a lawn mower. The man has his back to you, so no one holding the card can tell it's not Ba, no one who doesn't already know. He says I can be his secretary because I speak the best English. If you call us on the business phone, you will hear me say: "Hello, you have reached Tom's Professional Gardening Service. We are not here right now, but if you leave us a message, we will get back to you as soon as possible. Thank you."

It is hot and dusty where we live. Some people think it's dirty but they don't know much about us. They haven't seen our gardens full of lemongrass, mint, cilantro, and basil. Driving by with their windows rolled up, they've only seen the pigeons pecking at day-old rice and the skinny cats and dogs sitting in the skinny shade of skinny trees. Have they seen the berries that we pick, that turn our lips and fingertips red? How about the small staircase Ba built from our bedroom window to the backyard so I would have a shortcut to the clothesline? How about the Great Wall of China that snakes like a river from the top of the steep hill off Crandall Drive to the slightly curving bottom? Who has seen this?

It was so different at the Green Apartment. We had to close the gate behind us every time we came in. It clanged heavily, and I imagined a host of eyes, upstairs and down, staring at me from behind slightly parted curtains. There were four palm trees planted at the four corners of the courtyard and a central staircase that was narrow at the top and broad at the bottom. The steps were covered in fake grass, like the set of an old Hollywood movie, the kind that stars an aging beauty who wakes up to find something is terribly wrong.

We moved out of the Green Apartment after we turned on the TV one night and heard that our manager and his brother had hacked a woman to pieces and dumped the parts of her body into the Pacific Ocean in ten-gallon garbage bags that washed up onshore. Ma said she didn't want to live in a place haunted by a murdered lady. So we moved to Linda Vista, where she said there were a lot of Vietnamese people like us, people whose only sin was a little bit of gambling and sucking on fish bones and laughing hard and arguing loudly.

Ma shaved her head in Linda Vista because she got mad at Ba for gambling away her money and getting drunk every week during *Monday Night Football*. Ba gave her a blue baseball cap to wear until her hair grew back and she wore it backward, like a real badass.

After that, some people in Linda Vista said that Ma was

crazy and Ba was crazy for staying with her. But what do some people know?

When the photograph came, Ma and Ba got into a fight. Ba threw the fish tank out the front door and Ma broke all the dishes. They said they never should've got together.

Ma's sister sent her the photograph from Vietnam. It came in a stiff envelope. There was nothing else inside, as if anything more would be pointless. Ma held the photograph in her hands. She started to cry. "Child," she sobbed, over and over again. She wasn't talking about me. She was talking about herself.

Ba said, "Don't cry. Your parents have forgiven you."

Ma kept crying anyway and told him not to touch her with his gangster hands. Ba clenched his hands into tight fists and punched the walls.

"What hands?! What hands?!" he yelled. "Let me see the gangster! Let me see his hands!" I see his hands punch hands punch hands punch blood.

Ma is in the kitchen. She has torn the screen off the window. She is punctuating the pavement with dishes, plates, cups, rice bowls. She sends them out like birds gliding through the sky with nowhere in particular to go. Until they crash. Then she exhales "Huh!" in satisfaction.

I am in the hallway gulping air. I breathe in the breaking and the bleeding. When Ba plunges his hands into the fish tank, I detect the subtle tint of blood in water. When he throws the fish tank out the front door, yelling, "Let me see the gangster!" I am drinking up the spilt water and swallowing whole the beautiful tropical fish, their brilliant colors gliding across my tongue, before they can hit the ground, to cover themselves in dirt until only the whites of their eyes remain, blinking at the sun.

All the hands are in my throat, cutting themselves on broken dishes, and the fish swim in circles; they can't see for all the blood.

Ba jumps in his truck and drives away.

When I grow up I am going to be the gangster we are all looking for.

The neighborhood kids are standing outside our house, staring in through the windows and the open door. Even Anh, the chicken egg girl. I'm sure their gossiping mothers have sent them to spy on us. I run out front and dance like a crazy lady, dance like a fish, wiggle my head and whip my body around. At first they laugh but then they stop, not knowing what to think. Then I stop to stare them down, each one of them.

"What're you looking at?" I ask.

"Lookin' at you," one boy says, half giggling.

"Well," I say, with my hand on my hip, my head cocked to one side, "I'm looking at you too," and I give him my evil one-eyed look, focusing all my energy into my left eye. I stare at him hard as if my eye is a bullet and he can be dead.

I turn my back on them and walk into the house.

Ma is sitting in the window frame. The curve of her back is inside the bedroom while the rest of her body hangs outside, on the first of the steps Ba built from the bedroom to the garden. Without turning to look at me, she says, "Let me lift you into the attic."

"Why?"

"We have to move your grandparents in."

I don't really know what she is talking about, but I say O.K. anyway.

We have never needed the attic for anything. In fact, we have never gone up there. When we moved my grandparents in, Ma simply lifted me up and I pushed open the attic door with one hand while, with the other, I slipped the stiff envelope with the photograph of my grandparents into the crawl space above. I pushed the envelope the length of my arm and down to my fingertips. I pushed it so far it was beyond reach. Ma said that was all right; they had come to live with us, and sometimes you don't need to see or touch people to know they're there.

Ba came home drunk that night and asked to borrow my blanket. I heard him climbing the tree in the backyard.

It took him a long time. He kept missing the wooden blocks that run up the tree like a ladder. Ba had put them in himself when he built the steps going from the bedroom window into the garden. If you stood on the very top block, your whole body would be hidden by tree branches. Ba put those blocks in for me, so I could win at hide-and-go-seek.

When Ba had finally made it onto the roof, he lay down over my room and I could hear him rolling across my ceiling. Rolling and crying. I was scared he would roll off the edge and kill himself, so I went to wake Ma.

She was already awake. She said it would be a good thing if he rolled off. But later I heard someone climb the tree, and all night two bodies rolled across my ceiling. Slowly and firmly they pressed against my sleep, the Catholic schoolgirl and the Buddhist gangster, two dogs chasing each other's tails. They have been running like this for so long, they have become one dog, one tail.

Without any hair and looking like a man, my mother is still my mother, though sometimes I can't see her even when I look and look and look so long all the colors of the world begin to swim and bob around me. Her hands always bring me up, her big peasant hands with the flat, wide nails, wide like her nose and just as expressive. I will know her by her hands and by her walk, at once slow and urgent, the walk of a woman going to market with her goods bound securely to her side. Even walking empty-handed, my mother's gait suggests invisible bundles whose contents no one but she can reveal. And if I never see her again, I will know my mother by the smell of the sea salt and the prints of my own bare feet crossing sand, running to and away from, to and away from, family.

When the eviction notice came, we didn't believe it so we threw it away. It said we had a month to get out. The houses on our block had a new owner who wanted to tear everything down and build better housing for the community. It said we were priority tenants for the new complex, but we couldn't afford to pay the new rent so it didn't matter. The notice also said that if we didn't get out in time, all our possessions would be confiscated in accordance with some section of a law book or manual we were supposed to have known about but had never seen. We couldn't believe the eviction notice so we threw it away.

The fence is tall, silver, and see-through. Chain-link, it rattles when you shake it and wobbles when you lean against it. It circles our block like a bad dream. It is not funny like the clothesline whose flying shirts and empty pants suggest human birds and vanishing acts. This fence presses sharply against your brain. We three stand still as posts. Looking at it, then at one another—this side and that—out of the corners of our eyes. What are we thinking?

At night we come back with three uncles. Ba cuts a hole in the fence and we step through. Quiet, we break into our own house through the back window. Quiet, we steal back everything that is ours. We fill ten-gallon garbage bags with clothes, pots and pans, flip-flops, the porcelain figure of Mary, the wooden Buddha and the Chinese fisherman lamp. In the arc of our flashlights we find our favorite hairbrushes behind bedposts. When we are done, we clamber, breathless. Though it's quiet, we can hear police cars coming to get us.

We tumble out the window like people tumbling across continents. We are time traveling, weighed down by heavy furniture and bags of precious junk. We find ourselves leaning against Ba's yellow truck. Ma calls his name, her voice reaching like a hand feeling for a tree trunk in darkness.

In the car, Ma starts to cry. "What about the sea?" she asks. "What about the garden?" Ba says we can come back in the morning and dig up the stalks of lemongrass and fold the sea into a blue square. Ma is sobbing. She is beating the dashboard with her fists. "I want to know," she says, "I want to know, I want to know . . . who is doing this to us?" Hiccupping she says, "I want to know, why—why there's always a fence. Why there's always someone on the outside wanting someone . . . something on the inside and between them . . . this . . . sharp fence. Why are we always leaving like this?"

Everyone is quiet when Ma screams.

"Take me back!" she says. "I can't go with you. I've

forgotten my mother and father. I can't believe . . . Anh Minh, we've left them to die. Take me back."

Ma wants Ba to stop the car, but Ba doesn't know why. The three uncles, sitting in a row in the bed of the truck, think Ma is crazy. They yell in through the rear window, "My, are you going to walk back to Vietnam?"

"Yeah, are you going to walk home to your parents' house?"

In the silence another shakes his head and reaches into his shirt pocket for his cigarettes.

Ba puts his foot on the gas pedal. Our car jerks forward, and then plunges down the Crandall Drive hill. Ma says, "I need air, water . . ." I roll the window down. She puts her head in her hands. She keeps crying, "Child." Outside, I see the Great Wall of China. In the glare of the streetlamps, it is just a long strip of cardboard.

In the morning, the world is flat. Westinghouse Street is lying down like a jagged brushstroke of sun-burnt yellow. There is a big sign within the fence that reads

COMING SOON:

CONDOMINIUMS

TOWN HOUSES

FAMILY HOMES

Below these words is a copy of a watercolor drawing of a large pink complex.

. . .

We stand on the edge of the chain-link fence, sniffing the air for the scent of lemongrass, scanning this flat world for our blue sea. A wrecking ball dances madly through our house. Everything has burst wide open and sunk down low. Then I hear her calling them. She is whispering, "Ma/Ba, Ma/Ba." The whole world is two butterfly wings rubbing against my ear.

Listen . . . they are sitting in the attic, sitting like royalty. Shining in the dark, buried by a wrecking ball. Paper fragments floating across the surface of the sea.

There is not a trace of blood anywhere except here, in my throat, where I am telling you all this.

the bones of birds

After I had left Linda Vista, I was on the street when I ran into someone from home. I crossed the street when this man called me, called my name. I let that name fall all around me, never once sticking to me, even when he yelled, "You liar! I know it's you." I kept moving as the lilting syllables of my own name fell around me like licks of flame that extinguished on contact, never catching.

It was my father who taught me how to do this, how to keep moving even when a bone in the leg was broken or a muscle in the chest was torn. Growing up, there were nights when I would hear him staggering in the alley outside my bedroom window. I listened as he tackled the air, wrestled invisible enemies to the ground, punched his own shadow. Drunkenly, he would yell, "I'm not scared! Come out and fight me. I'm here!"

Some nights, he was so long and loud out there, the old woman upstairs would open her window and yell down, "We don't care! Let us sleep!" My father mumbled in response a threat to kill us all with one shot. I lay in bed and pictured the lonely bullet threading its way through the entire apartment building, lifting each of us out of bed and drawing us closer in our sleep. I imagined our waking the next morning to find ourselves each pierced at the very center, our bodies pulled tightly together and suspended against the blue sky, like a string of fish Ba hoists high from one end.

In the fall of the year I turned sixteen, I jumped out my bedroom window and ran away. The night's black roads wound like long stretches of river. Streetlamps stood to either side and hung their heads as I ran past. Cars crouched in driveways. Garbage cans lined the edge of the sidewalks, ready for the morning pickup. Other than the sudden shriek of two cats fighting in an alley, the night was calm. I ran until I could feel my heart pounding in my throat. Then I stood in the middle of the street and listened to my breath. When I got cold, I drew my arms back through the sleeves of my T-shirt and wrapped them around myself for warmth. I was barefoot, empty-handed, small and light as a leaf. The streets ribboned out in all directions. I lifted one foot and then the other, ready to run down all of them.

It was spring when the man saw me; the jacarandas bloomed, blanketing the sidewalks with small purple flowers. I felt that I had to continue running, at least through the summer. I hadn't yet found a way to return to where my parents waited, in that house that was on fire. As it turned out, I ran past the summer and into another fall, another spring, another summer, and I kept on running.

What season was it when I woke, in that one-room apartment, thousands of miles away from the streets where I'd grown up? It was early morning and the sun was rising. I lay in bed and listened as, four stories below me, the garbage collectors dragged the trash cans to the curb. I watched, through an open window, as the shadows of tree branches flickered across the face of the redbrick building across the street. When the sun shined directly on the bricks, they seemed to jump from the building and hang together in the air, like a red sheet, hovering. I closed my eyes and imagined running through the sheet but as I approached, the sheet became a wall of red and from somewhere deep inside it, I heard the sound of my father's voice calling.

.   .   .

I have a black-and-white photograph of him at sixteen, in which he wears a hat of canvas camouflage cocked to one side. His expression is wary. His arms are crossed in front of him, bare and luminous, one hand balled into a fist. In this picture, what reveals him most is the will to give nothing away.

The rumors about him are mysterious and mundane. Before he was my father, he was a skinny kid in the South Vietnamese army. He was a heroin addict. He was a gangster. He sold American cigarettes on the black market. He cruised girls. He ran away from home. He was part of a select unit trained by the Americans. He jumped out of airplanes and disappeared for weeks into the jungles and hill towns. His friends fell around him, first during the war and then after the war, but somehow he alone managed to crawl here, on his hands and knees, to this life.

From what I'd heard, I pictured my father wearing a fedora because gangsters wore fedoras; my father pointing a gun toward dark fields because it wasn't clear to me whom he would be shooting; my father disappearing down an alley, escaping his own father, like me fast and light on his feet; my father slumped in the corner of a windowless room, strung out, in a cold sweat as I had found him one day.

. . .

My young father lifting me in his arms, his smiling face moving across mine like so much sunlight. A quick kiss on my forehead before he hands me to my mother, to an aunt, to a grandparent, to a neighbor. My body swinging between one pair of arms toward another. I am on my feet again, standing, watching my father leave. I feel the heat of the dusty road rising toward my calves. It almost tickles, this heat. My father is going away somewhere and all I can remember is how a branch of a coconut tree was lifted from its trunk by a warm breeze coming from the beach that day. How this branch seemed to sigh. Once. Twice. How it seemed to wave at me.

Early memories of my father are always of his leaving. He didn't live with us, was only, my mother would remind my older brother and me in her steady voice, visiting. He was in the South Vietnamese army and was stationed either in the city or in the country but never near our coastal town. I understood that I, even more than my brother, looked like him. The women would say, "You have his eyes, his nose, his dark skin, his silence." When I was angry, my mother would say I had his poisonous temper. When I was good, she would laugh and say I had his charm. Some nights she would pull me to her and stare intently into my face. Then, holding me at arm's length, my mother would turn me from side to side studying my face from one angle and then another. In this way, she tried to divine all the answers to her questions about his well-being. As though floating just beneath my own gaze was the reflection of my father, hundreds of dark miles away.

The night I left Vietnam, it was my father who carried me down to the beach and placed me on the fishing boat. During hours that must have been ones of fear, anxiety, and desperation, my only memory is of how calmly I sat waiting for him.

He'd gone back to get my mother and the rest of our family but as it was rumored that someone had alerted the police, the escape plan unraveled in chaos and he couldn't find her anywhere. In a panic, he returned to the boat hoping she would have found her own way there, only to realize, as it pulled away from the shore, that my mother's must have been among the many voices, each calling for help as he passed by in the water.

Years later, even after our family was reunited, my father would remember those voices as a seawall between Vietnam and America or as a kind of floating net, each voice linked to the next by a knot of grief.

In America, my father worked as a house painter and then a welder. After he'd been laid off from his welding job, he became a gardener. He sent me to the local library to check out books about plants and trees for him. Together we looked through the books and learned that the tree that closed its leaves at night was called a mimosa. There were many varieties of palm trees. Among them, the Alexandra, the Australian feather, the betel-nut, the book, the broom, the coconut, the date, the dwarf, the fern, the fishtail, the wine, and the walking stick.

My father noted that, as in southern Vietnam, bougainvillea and eucalyptus thrived in the climate of southern California. Cactuses had blooms to rival those of roses but few of his customers wanted a cactus garden. They insisted on green lawns even in the middle of summer droughts. It was his job to give them what they wanted, such as he could. He installed sprinkler systems, trimmed hedges, swept walkways, raked up fallen leaves and hauled away broken tree branches. My father and the people he worked for rarely saw each other. He would come to their homes after they'd left for work in the morning and was sure to leave before they returned in the evening. So long as he kept the grass green, there was no reason for them to meet.

At the end of the day, he stood outside the front door of our apartment and dusted the dirt off his clothes and shoes before coming inside. He would bring home bruised roses from the gardens he tended and, emptying his pockets onto the dining room table, he would announce, "Lemons! Oranges! Kumquats! For sale!"

. . .

I used to watch his eyes take in a room, insinuate their way deep into and through corners, walls. If I were sitting across from him, he would stare at a point on the wall behind me, his eyes moving like an arrow through my hair, pinning me to my place.

He would gaze beyond a person's shoulder as though watching storm clouds gather on the horizon. Neither holding the clouds back nor inviting them on, his eyes merely took in their approach. More than once I have seen people talking with him turn around to see what was behind them.

The year I left home, my father and I would sit at the kitchen table in the evenings and pass the silence back and forth, like a smoke.

"It's hot."

"Yes."

"Another fire."

"So many lately."

"Where was this one?"

"In a canyon."

"Are you hungry?"

"Ate already."

"Tired?"

"Not so tired."

"I'm going to read."

"Here?"

"In my room."

"Brighter in there."

"It's dark out here."

"Yes, it's late now."

"You want some light?"

"No."

I'd go to my room and leave him sitting in the dusky half-light. Where he would go in his mind, I don't know. Eventually my mother would come home from her restaurant job or from grocery shopping. She would walk around the house turning on all the lights, and my father would stand up from the kitchen table to greet her. "I lost track of the time," he'd say as if to explain the darkness.

What happened during those hours when I sat in the fishing boat and waited for my father to return? Were they hours or only one hour? Or one half of one hour? It was after sundown. We were escaping so we needed darkness. But I don't remember darkness and I don't remember light. I was waiting in the boat, and the boat filled with people; but I remember no one other than my father. He walked slowly toward me, gently pushing everyone else aside. He picked me up and kissed my hair. He stroked my face and rocked me, even though I wasn't crying. The boat must have cut into the water as it pulled away from the shore. But I don't remember the sound of the water and I don't remember the shape of the shore. Is this because of the darkness?

Or is it because we didn't turn around once to look at the lights of our town? My father stared ahead, at the stars, and at the moon, which was half full and half vanished.

That first night at the refugee camp in Singapore, we lay in a hammock outside trying to sleep. I had closed my eyes to the moon and was listening to the sound of the crickets—a hum that would stop and start at odd intervals. Amid these darting sounds, I began to make out one other, the sound of someone crying. Soon the sound seemed so constant that I pictured a flood of tears rushing toward us. I thought that if the tears touched us, my father and I would spill out of our bodies, dissolve, and fall through the netting of the hammock.

Frightened, I opened my eyes and stared hard at my father's back. When I touched a finger to his spine, he curled upon himself like an anemone. It was then, as he pulled away from me, that I realized the crying came from him. The hammock tilted toward the ground, the crickets went quiet, a dark cloud crossed the face of the moon, and time stopped.

Time stopped.

Then—inexplicably, incredibly—it continued.

NEIGHBORHOOD NEWS: A Vietnamese man and a young girl were seen wandering the aisles of the Safeway Supermarket on University Avenue between the hours of midnight and 1 a.m.

According to the store manager, their behavior was "strange" but not in any way threatening. When asked to clarify, the manager explained, "Everything seemed to interest them. I mean, everything, from the TV dinners to the 10-pound bags of dog food."

The man was seen picking up various items—a pack of shoelaces, a pine-tree car freshener, a box of Jell-O, a Pyrex measuring cup—and studying them. According to other customers and store employees, he would then show the items to the girl and encourage her to hold them for a minute before he carefully returned them to the shelf.

From the random way they went through the store, it was clear they were not looking for anything in particular. They made no purchases and left shortly before 1 a.m., after the child, who was perhaps his daughter, lay down in the spice aisle while the man was absorbed with the different varieties of salt available.

They were last seen walking east toward Orange Street. The man was carrying the girl who—having stayed up long past her bedtime—had fallen fast asleep.

Whenever we couldn't sleep during those two years before Ma arrived, Ba and I would go for walks around the neighborhood and stop to look at the window displays. We stood in front of Ken's admiring the many shining pairs of dress-up shoes, each positioned at such an angle as to suggest the wearer had floated out of them, while the shoes, too heavy to follow, had to stay behind. The desk in the window of Smith's Stationery store had two fountain pens on it, as well as a jar of finely sharpened pencils, a memo pad with a list of things to do and a single, hard line drawn through the things that had been done. Sheets of stationery were displayed like an open fan or a hand of cards. At the top right-hand corner of the desk was a stack of envelopes of different sizes and different colors with a letter opener lying ready nearby.

What interested us most were the headless, footless, armless mannequins of Dora's Fine Apparel. They wore shirts that stretched snuggly across their torsos and tucked neatly into their pressed pants. Leather belts cinched their waists and we could see, by the way the fabric of a trouser leg draped over their thighs or the way a flowered skirt hung from their hips, that if these mannequins were people, they would be the kind with straight white teeth and no bones, only muscles. With their puffed-up chests and crisp clothes, they exuded an air of confidence that impressed us.

. . .

After studying the window displays, we would cut down an alley behind Dora's and walk over to the Mexican bakery. It was a French bakery but we called it the Mexican bakery because the baker was a Mexican. He was a short and stocky man with a little mustache and every night he wore the same thing: a white V-neck T-shirt and a long white apron over blue jeans. We would stand in the shadows outside the open back door and watch him work. He listened to English-language tapes and repeated aloud the sentences and phrases as he moved around the kitchen. "Hello," he said to a bag of flour, before he lifted it off the ground and carried it to the counter. "How are you?" he asked the counter, clearing it with the palm of his hand. Of the measuring cup he asked, "Where is the train station?" Kneading the dough, he said, "Thank you very much." And then, "You are so very welcome." Shaping the dough into croissants, he asked, "What is the weather like in Orlando?" His voice softly rolling the *r* before touching down briefly on the *d*.

If after visiting the Mexican baker we still weren't sleepy, we'd wander the aisles of the supermarket or ride the fluorescent-lit city bus as it rolled from our neighborhood through the darkened downtown, onto the empty highway, and out to the beach. The bus lurched like a boat at every stop and we'd sit with our faces pressed against the glass, taking in the ghost town of 3 a.m. The streets, with their closed shops, and sleeping houses, their wrecked cars and swaying palm trees, their hungry stray dogs and staggering bums, their 24-hour check-cashing windows and upended grocery carts, would all glide past us. At the end of the line, we'd step off the bus, sniff the salt air, and then get back on the bus again.

For the return trip, we sat on the opposite side of the bus and watched as the streets were cleaned by teams of men in green jumpsuits, some of them pushing long brooms across the sidewalks as others drove the cleaning trucks that foamed soapy water at the mouth. By the time we got home, the sun would be up and little birds would be darting in and out of the bushes, screaming their heads off.

After Ma arrived, our family moved from one apartment building to another before finally settling in Linda Vista. It was there that my father made his closest friend, a Vietnamese man down the street with whom he would sit on the front steps in the evenings, and talk about the past. They agreed that the past was when they were young and in Vietnam. So young they still believed that if a beautiful girl—riding by on a bicycle—offered so much as a sidelong glance, it was reason enough to chase after her.

Sipping bottles of beer, they talked about the war and how it was their youth and how when it ended it was like waking from a long dream or a long nightmare. And now the war was in the past. Chewing on salted peanuts, they talked about how certain foods were in the past and certain smells. For example, the smoky smell of dried cuttlefish as it was being roasted over a charcoal stove. And the smell of the first rain after the dry season. They watched as cars drove by and my father remembered the rivers crowded with fishing boats and the children who sat cross-legged on the floor of those boats, mending their families' nets. As evening approached, they talked about heat as something that was in the past, as well as certain fruits. The dragon fruit, for instance. The sky turned indigo above them, and as they stood up to wish each other goodnight, my father and his friend agreed that certain colors also seemed to have vanished. Like red. Red was in the past.

He used to walk around the house and mutter the spelling of his name in English.

"M-I-"

"M-I-N-"

"M-I-N-H"

He pronounced the *H* like a combination of "ache" and "ash": "aycsh." He would point his finger at the air, as if each letter were appearing briefly before him, suspended for a moment, as he awaited the next. But before he could spell out his whole name, the letter preceding the one to appear would often be gone. Like a blind man circling a small room, searching for but always missing the door that led to the hallway, the streets, the open air, he would repeat each letter of his name over and over again, in a tone more hushed and halting than the time before. Even when he was able to spell out his whole name, he couldn't quite trust that this was he himself. Were these the letters? Was this his name?

Late at night, unable to sleep after having moved from his bed to the couch to four dining room chairs lined up in a row, he drives down to the beach and spins the car wheels in the wet sand, daring himself to drive into the sea. At daybreak he drives the car home, parks it at the edge of the driveway, lowers the seat, and falls asleep, exhausted.

He starts digging a trench around the base of a palm tree in the garden of one of the people he works for. He digs until his hands bleed. When he remembers that no one has asked him to do this, he packs up his equipment, pulls the lawn mower into the truck bed and drives away. Let them call. Let them curse into the answering machine. He will never go back to that house again.

Too drunk to drive from a friend's house and too proud to be driven, he decides to walk the six blocks home. He walks with one foot on the sidewalk and the other foot on the road. It makes him feel like a crippled soldier marching far behind the troops. Every third step, he shouts out his own name and the order "Stand up straight! Stand up straight, now!"

He becomes prone to rages. He smashes televisions, VCRs, chases friends and family down the street, brandishing hammers and knives in broad daylight. Then from night until early morning he sits on the couch in the living room, his body absolutely still, his hands folded on his lap, penitent. He sits in that position for hours, graced by the darkness, straining toward things no one can see.

I grew up studying my father so closely as to suggest I was certain I saw my future in him. I would inherit his lithe figure and beautiful smile. I would build and break things with my hands. I would answer to names not my own and be ordered around like a child. I would disappear into every manner of darkness only to awaken amid a halo of faces encircling my body. Shame would crush me. I would turn away from the people I loved. I would regard with suspicion the bare shoulders of a woman I desired. The sight of two boys shooting marbles in a dirt yard would fill me with sadness. I would drink to lies about the past. I would beg the dead to come for me. The sight of a young girl playing house, sweeping out an imaginary courtyard with a branch of eucalyptus, and the little song she sang, about a fluttering butterfly, and the way her arm described the course of its body in flight, would haunt me.

Whereas my father would disappear into himself when haunted, I would leap out of windows and run. If there were no windows, I would kick down doors. The point was to get to the street, at any cost. I would come to see running as inseparable from living. I would choose falling asleep on rooftops and on the lawns of strangers to lying in my own bed, surrounded by knots of memories I had no language with which to unravel. Yet exactly like my father, I would become suspicious of tenderness and was calmest when I had one hand quietly lying over the other, both ready to be raised in an instant, shattering to the bone whatever dared come too near to me.

One night when my father was sitting on the couch looking sad and broken, he turned and realized there was someone standing where he had thought there was only a shadow. He came for me then because I had seen him. I leapt through a window and ran from the house, but before I could make it to the street, he caught me by my hair and pulled me back inside. Gripping my head with one hand, he raised the other and demanded to know what I had seen.

To protect myself, I tried to forget everything: that

first night at the refugee camp in Singapore; those early morning walks after we arrived in America; the sound of his voice asking a question no one could answer; the shapes his fists left along a wall; the bruises that blossomed on the people around him; the smell of the fruit he brought home from the gardens he tended; the way the air seemed charged with memories of blood; the nets we fell through, faster and faster, year after year, dreaming of land.

The only thing I couldn't drive away was the memory of my brother, whose body lay just beyond reach, forming the shape of a distant shore.

Before I had run away for good, my father once came to pick me up at a shelter. As we sat in a conference with two counselors, he was asked if there was anything he wanted to say. He shook his head. When pressed, he looked down at his hands. He apologized for what his hands had done. The counselors understood this to mean he was taking responsibility for his drunken rages. They nodded in approval. But then he drew his palms together and apologized for all that his hands had not been able to do. He spread his hands wide open, and said, in Vietnamese, to anyone who could understand, there were things he had lost a grasp of.

The room seemed to shrink in the face of his sorrow. Beside him the two counselors were like tight little shrubs no one had ever watered. I thought they had no right to frown at my father. I could not wait to get us out of there. I told the counselors that I was ready to go home. I remember crossing the parking lot, my hand in my father's hand, the two of us running to the car as though we were escaping together again.

After I ran away, I phoned my parents only a couple of times, to let them know I was all right. The last call was from the airport, to tell them that I was moving to the East Coast to go to school. My father wasn't home. My mother said, "The East Coast? But it's so cold and far away." She urged me to remain in San Diego. When I said I couldn't, she sighed. "I don't understand you," she said. We were silent. I listened to her breath. Then, as if I hadn't phoned but had walked through the front door and was now standing with her in the kitchen, Ma asked if I was hungry. The question was a familiar one; it was what my mother said in lieu of "I love you." I told her I had to go, the plane was boarding; and would she give my regards to Ba. She said that as soon as he returned from wherever he had gone to, she would tell him that his daughter had called.

Ba would often come to visit me in dreams. We would pick out shirts together. Feel this one, he says, brushing a soft sleeve against my cheek. In another dream, we sit across from each other at a corner table in a crowded café.

By the way we're sitting, with legs slightly apart, hands flat on our knees, torsos bent forward, and by the way we're laughing, first with our eyes and then our heads thrown back, it is clear to everyone around us that we have become each other. I dream we live in one room. It is a small room. We share a bed. As I am lying down to sleep, he is getting ready to leave. He sits down on the edge of the bed and I know, from the weight of his body, that he is leaving forever. I pretend to be asleep so he won't wake me to say good-bye. But because it is my dream, I see everything. He puts on one shoe and then the other, carefully tying the laces. He buttons his coat, a dark blue trench coat with epaulets that jut out. He takes his fedora off a nail on the wall, runs his fingers through his hair, and dons the hat. He picks up his keys from the bedside table and walks backward out of the room, his gaze moving from me, to the windows, the table, the floor and back to me again. He goes through the door without opening it. I remain in the room, both as the one feigning sleep and the one whose dream this is. As if from the sky of the dream, I glance at myself, then the windows, the table, the floor, and back again. I do this obsessively, pinning everything to its place.

The nightmare of my father's departure: Like a folding table, like a bed that jumps into the wall to be swallowed whole, I see my father's body disappearing. His elbows drawn in toward his stomach, his back bent like a bow. One leg, then the other steps backward and is gone. His shoulder blades fold—one into the other—like a pair of rented wings. His head rolls back onto his neck and I see that his eyes, once black and brilliant, are now empty of expression, like two pieces of volcanic rock that have been drowned in a river to cool.

The nightmare of my return: I find him sitting at the kitchen table, staring out the window. "Get up," I say. He doesn't answer. "Get up," I say, again. I've come to fight him. He knows this and doesn't look at me. I am furious. I can hardly stand still. He continues looking out the window and very slowly he slides his hands to the center of the table. They are covered in dirt and horribly swollen. They tremble as he lifts them from the table. It destroys me to see his hands like this. Ma enters, from another room. "I didn't know how to find you to tell you," she says, wringing her own hands.

Years after I ran away, my father managed to find me. I had not dreamed the phone call. I was standing at the sink, filling a blue-striped bowl with soap and water when the phone rang. Cradling the receiver against my ear, I heard my father say my name twice and then the word "Help" in English, followed by the word "Ba" in Vietnamese.

I turned the water off and leaned against the kitchen counter in stunned silence. Instinctively, I looked toward the window, but could not see out. The midday sun glared against the pane. I remember how dark the window frame looked against the glass, like four pieces of wood trying to hold back a fire.

I heard my father say that he was in trouble. He said the word "trouble" in English. In Vietnamese, he asked, "Do you understand?" "Yes," I said, and again, "Yes," and again "Yes." Three times, in Vietnamese.

What shook me? Was it the sound of his voice—reedy, high and thin? Or the fact that he was pleading? And then crying?

Or was it that I could say nothing—in any language—to make him stop.

Between us now there hangs the familiar smoke of small rooms crowded with people larger than their situation. People who, feeling they have no recourse to change the circumstances of their lives, fold down, crumble into their own shadows. This is what I saw my father do. He made himself small, so that in the world there was very little left of him, even while within me his hunger grew. It became expansive, billowing like an abandoned parachute searching the sky for the man who has fallen.

.   .   .

I fly over the streets and the stations that we passed through. I fly over the coastline of our town in Vietnam. I see the boat pulling away from the shore. The town doesn't vanish behind us; it merely recedes. I see us standing at the small fountain in that park in downtown San Diego. We are waiting among the sleeping homeless for the Federal Building to open so we can apply for our "papers." My father wets his hands in the fountain and rubs the sleep out of my eyes. I fly along Orange Street, cut over to University and circle the air above the Mexican bakery. I fly over the four blossoming lemon trees my father planted in the backyard of a house in La Jolla. I fly over Westinghouse Street and see the pink condominiums with their fenced-in swimming pools built after they kicked us out of our house and tore our block down. The smell of eucalyptus draws me toward a canyon. As I alight on the soft dirt of the canyon, I catch my father dancing.

One night, before Ma arrived, Ba took me to a party at the house of a friend of his down in Florida Canyon. Bored among the adults, I wandered outside. Slowly circling the house, I caught glimpses of the party as I passed each open window. I saw someone's necklace on the floor. I saw my father standing alone, his body swaying slightly from side to side. He had his hands down on either side of his hips and was moving them faster and faster, like the connecting rods of a locomotive getting ready to take off.

I saw a woman turn her head to look toward him. She smiled slowly. I saw him lift one foot and then the other, a soft stamping. I saw someone stand and walk toward the stereo. I heard the music go up. My father shook his head and almost laughed out loud as though he just couldn't believe how fast he was moving now; snaking beside rivers, tunneling through mountains, with each stamp of his foot the train whistle exclaiming, "I'm here and gone, here and gone, here and gone!"

I looked away, distracted by the sound of something stirring in the canyon. When I turned back, I saw my father standing quite still, struggling to remain on his feet. His eyes were closed and his body, leadened by drink, twitched, as if he felt suddenly surrounded. He gulped air, and after a while it became the rhythmic hiccupping of someone who has been sobbing for hours.

I stood outside, looking in through the open window. He looked small. I thought of the bones of birds. I thought of a prized pebble in my palm. I closed my hand into a fist and pressed it hard against my body.

nu'ó'c

My father was sitting at the kitchen table watching the evening news when the telephone began to ring. He turned up the volume on the television and focused on the images. It was summer in southern California and there were wildfires in forests and canyons across the state. He watched footage of firemen in orange suits, moving slowly and deliberately like so many lobsters, trying to hose down a flaming bank of trees. Above their heads, the sky filled with bursts of black smoke while, before them, the trees and the hill they were standing on burned calmly. Jets of water shot from the fire hoses and arced through the air. The phone continued to ring. My father picked up the remote again and changed the channel. More news. He watched footage of a flood in the middle of the country. A man and his son were traveling by canoe down the main street of their small town. The boy smiled and waved at the news cameras but the father's expression remained grim. The story changed. Two politicians in dark suits stood on a well-lit stage, shaking hands. Like the boy in the previous story, they waved at the news cameras. Somewhere below them, an audience was applauding. The story changed. A woman wearing a blue kerchief stood in a field of green grass. My father wondered if this was Europe. The phone continued to ring. My father thought the grass looked as lush as a rice paddy. The woman pointed to the ground and said something in a language my father didn't understand. The camera moved in closer. She continued pointing at the ground and then very slowly shook her head from side to side. For a moment, my father thought the footage was in slow motion. Then he decided, no, it was not. The phone continued to ring. He changed the channel. A baseball game: men adjusting their caps and spitting. He walked to the kitchen sink and filled a pot with water from the faucet. As he carried the water out the front door to water the potted plants on the stairs, the little dog he'd found wandering along the side of the highway last week came running out of the bedroom, and the phone stopped ringing.

Twenty years ago, my brother's body was pulled from the South China Sea and left lying on the beach to dry. Friends and relatives encircle him. Two young boys lean against each other, staring at my brother's body. One of the boys scratches the ankle of his left foot with the toes of his right foot. The uncle who dragged my brother out is squatting beside the body and breathing hard, exhausted. There is a hum of indecision. No one has yet begun to cry. The moment is warped, sensuous. It hovers like summer heat.

From down the beach, you can see my grandfather running. He approaches arms first, reaching through the circle of people to lift up my brother and carry him away. As he leaves the beach, my brother in his arms, my grandfather isn't running but he isn't walking either. Like a dark, wiry bird he seems to be hopping and then gliding across the hot sand. At our house he pushes open the thatched gate with the side of his foot and sends the chickens scattering. He carries my brother across the small courtyard, up the two steps, into the shade inside.

That night, as they did every night that season, the squid boats dotted the horizon. The lights the fishermen lit to lure the squids into the nets bobbed in and out of sight, troubled beacons. I sat up in bed and looked out the window at the lights on the water. The sight of them always calmed me when I couldn't sleep. But that night, I lay back down and stared through the mosquito netting at my brother's body. It was like magic, how still he lay. It impressed me and I tried to lie as still as he. Women were gathered in the courtyard crying. I wished that they would be quiet and that someone would turn down the oil lamps, so my brother and I could sleep.

In Linda Vista, my father moved up and down the steps to the apartment, watering the potted plants. There were three jasmine, a couple of pepper plants, an ornamental orange tree and a desert rose. He had planted the desert rose three years before and was happy to see it was now beginning to bud. As he watered the plants, his thoughts went back to the news. The woman standing in the field of grass—what was she shaking her head about? And why was she alone? He remembered a view of mountains in the distance behind her. He picked dead leaves from the jasmine plants. He remembered the firemen and thought about how after a fire or a flood a camera crew would follow a family as they walked through what was left of their home. Tomorrow evening's news might show some man or woman pointing out the charred remains of a stairwell, or a hole in the ceiling, or a waterlogged floor. Occasionally, the camera lingered on the view from a window, of trees curled on the ground, their roots raised against the sky or a hillside, black and barren. It was these shots that stayed with him the longest.

.   .   .

The little dog was on the landing at the top of the stairs. It was chasing its tail and then jumping up on its hind legs. He remembered when he first saw the dog. It was early morning and he was on his way to a gardening job. As he drove along the highway, he came across a hillside covered in goldenrod and wildflowers. Dew glistened on every-thing so that even the ice plant looked lush, more alive.

He was looking at the flowers, and then he saw the dog. It was one of those small, white ones that barked a lot and didn't run very fast. It was running back and forth on the side of the road, barking at the cars as if it was protecting the entire hillside from them. He didn't know from what direction the dog had come and but for his feeling that the dog had somehow emerged from the hillside, he might not have pulled over and called to it.

When he walked back inside the apartment and heard the roar of a crowd, he realized—as if for the first time—how loud the television was. With his finger pressing down on the volume-lowering button, he watched two seconds of the baseball game. A ball was shooting through the air, moving at 100 mph, when he turned the TV off.

My mother stood in the courtyard of the house in Viet-nam. It was night. She was surrounded by women crying and whispering about my brother. They told my mother that my grandfather had made a terrible mistake carrying the boy into the house. They said that my brother—they called him "the boy"—was full of "bad water" and now that the water had been brought inside the house, it was too late, and if my mother wasn't careful, they said, pointing their fingers at her, she would lose all her children to the "bad water." "That's enough!" my grandfather said. "Why don't you busybodies go home?"

It was dark but they could see him standing in the doorway, his figure lit from behind by the oil lamps on the family altar. He called for my mother to come inside. The women hushed themselves and slipped away, leaving my mother standing alone in the courtyard.

She closed her eyes and listened as the sound of the women's footsteps digging into the sand slowly faded. When she couldn't hear them anymore, she turned and looked toward the house. She thought about my father who was being held in a reeducation camp. She heard a noise and her eyes darted to the thatched gate at the entrance to the courtyard. It was one of her mother's chickens pulling on a piece of straw. Why wasn't her husband there, impatiently pushing open the thatched gate, running across the courtyard to find her?

She walked to the well at the side of the house and, placing her hands on its lip, she leaned forward and looked down. It was too dark to see anything. She picked up the empty water bucket and, with all her strength, threw it down into the well. She remembered how, as a girl, she liked to watch the bucket dance on the rope as it dropped into the darkness of the well. What had delighted her then was the way the bucket hit the water, tipped over on its side, slowly filled with water until—too heavy to float—it disappeared.

The rope went taut against her hand. It now sickened her to picture the bucket filling with water. She pressed her left leg against the well for leverage and began to pull ferociously, bringing the bucket up faster than she had ever done before. She wrapped her arms around the bucket of water and clung to it. As she lifted it the weight was comforting, but when she saw her own face reflected in the water, she immediately felt betrayed. She set the bucket down on the lip of the well, took a step back and stared at it. Then she leaned forward and, placing the palms of both her hands against the bucket, she shoved it down the well. Once it had hit the bottom and sunk, she pulled it back up again. This time, she didn't bother to set the bucket on the lip of the well; she simply gripped it with two hands and, holding it high over the mouth of the well, she let it drop straight down. The full bucket slapped the water and as the sound of this echoed up to her, she was filled with a violent sense of pleasure. She thought the sound should never stop.

She heard her name and turned to see her father standing in the courtyard. His arms looked impossibly long and he was holding them out toward her. She thought of how in those very arms he had carried her son home that afternoon. Was it true, what the women had said, about the boy's body being filled with bad water? She turned to look at her father and all she could see was the image of him running, his arms empty, his hands cupped before him, spilling blood and water. She shook her head slowly from side to side trying to erase this image of him but she could not. When he called to her once more, she ran past him and into the house.

My father sat on the edge of the bed in San Diego. The curtain was drawn across the window and the room was dark. He heard the little dog eating from its bowl out on the patio off the kitchen. He glanced at the clock on the dresser—9:30. At midnight, he would drive downtown to pick up my mother from the restaurant where she worked. He couldn't remember the name of the place. It was one of those Vietnamese restaurants that had a French word in its name. Even its décor was meant to evoke the colonial era, as though that was when life was best in Vietnam. This somehow allowed them to sell bowls of pho for fifteen, sometimes twenty dollars to Americans who seemed charmed by the ceiling fans, wicker chairs, and banquettes covered in prints of flowering frangipani. He wanted to tell the Americans who ate there that in many ways, a bowl of pho was not much different from a bowl of chicken noodle soup. Pho tasted better but nothing to warrant paying twenty dollars. That's why no Vietnamese people ate at this restaurant.

My mother was a cook there. My father thought she didn't get paid what she deserved. This was the main reason he didn't like the place. When he told her so, she said, "Why don't you buy me a restaurant and I'll leave theirs?" He told her he couldn't do that for her just yet but offered her a job gardening with him. She thought it was a joke and laughed.

They'd been sitting at the kitchen table, drinking iced coffee. Laughing, she stirred her coffee with a long spoon and said, "You're very particular. I would be afraid of watering the plants wrong." He said, "How could you water the plants wrong?" "I'm sure I'd find a way," she said, crunching on a piece of ice.

He set the alarm on the clock, took off his shoes and lay down on the bed, without turning down the covers. He would nap for exactly half an hour. He closed his eyes and pictured himself and my mother in their old age, pushing around barrels of dirt and planting seeds to grow a garden. The thought of the garden pleased him. He pictured it being in one of those towns he had passed through during the war, a town far from the town they had lived in in Vietnam. He fell asleep thinking about a place deep in the countryside miles from the sight or the sound or the smell of the sea.

.   .   .

The next evening, after mass, the women returned to the courtyard. They told my mother that they had come to pray for the boy but that they couldn't come into the house. There were about fifteen of them and they stood around the steps, chanting their prayers. The chickens walked back and forth behind them, stopping now and then to scratch at the ground.

Inside the house, my brother lay on a straw mat at the center of the room. My mother, grandmother, aunts and uncles sat or stood around him, their shoulders hunched and their eyes blank. I was sitting on my grandfather's lap, in a corner of the room. Every now and then I would look out the window, at the women chanting on the steps. Some of their mouths were stained bright red from chewing on betel nuts. I looked up at my grandfather and saw his furrowed forehead and his mouth slightly open. I thought he was going to say something, maybe tell my brother to get up, but he didn't.

By the time the women finished their chanting it was dark out. I stood with my grandfather on the steps of the house and watched as the women crossed the courtyard in a group. We could hear the waves breaking on the beach.

The sky was dark and full of stars. I pushed at my grand-father's arm and asked him to pull a star down for me. This was a game of ours. I thought he might not want to play that night but he reached up, grabbed at the air and brought his fingertips down to touch the center of my palm. "There," he said, slowly spreading his fingers open. As soon as he pulled his hand away, I made a fist closing my hand onto the star. I put my hands behind my back and passed the star from one to the other. Then I threw it over my shoulder the way I'd seen the older kids do with a loose tooth, over their shoulders and onto the roofs of their houses for good luck. But instead of throwing the star onto the roof, I threw it into our house, aiming blindly for my brother. I counted to five, and then I glanced over my shoulder to see whether he had moved.

My father lay in bed in Linda Vista and listened to the phone ring. The small white dog was jumping up and down at the foot of the bed. He imagined that the sound of the phone ringing was the invisible charge that sent the dog flying straight up into the air and that the intervals of silence between each ring were what brought the dog down again. If he focused hard enough on the dog, he could almost forget that the phone was actually ringing because someone was calling for him.

. . .

A man in uniform is talking with my mother on the steps of the house in Vietnam. My grandmother inside the house calls out to my mother to invite the man in. My mother doesn't do it. Instead, she fixes her eyes on the man and says, "I know there was a war, but it's over now. Why can't you let him go?" The man says, "We can't tell you that. Your husband knows about the boy but he won't be able to attend the . . . He asked me to tell you to bury the boy and—" "Go," my mother says, pointing her finger toward the road. "Go. I don't want to bury the boy. I don't want to bury the boy by myself," she says, her voice rising. "I want you to let my husband go. I want him to come back. And help me bury the boy."

The man can see that she is upset. He senses that she is either going to cry or strike him or both. He looks past her and is relieved to see my grandmother walking out of the house, toward them. He hears the old woman muttering, "Child, oh child," and finds the cracked note in her voice, combined with the heat of the courtyard and the sight of the chickens busily scratching the ground around his feet, unbearable. One of the chickens pecks at his ankle and he makes to kick at it but before he can, it disappears behind the well.

He looks at the young woman. She is probably the same age as his wife was when they first met. He wants to tell her there is nothing to do now but to bury her son and be patient. A whole country has to be rebuilt. Does she expect everything to stop simply because she hadn't taken care to keep her own child from wandering too far into the water? He sees the women, the mother standing with her hand on her daughter's shoulder. How many times has he seen this? He looks away. He doesn't say anything.

The young woman pushes a strand of hair away from her face and he notices her high cheekbones and the dark beauty of her eyes. Before, he'd seen only her anger and frustration. Now there was something resolute about her expression, as if she could see exactly what her situation was. She looked him in the face and, with a fury that surprised him, said, "Leave. Leave this house."

The phone was ringing and my father was afraid that instead of the usual telemarketers offering credit cards, it was someone calling from Vietnam. His fear was vivid and though probably unfounded, it pinned him to the bed like a weight. He imagined the moment as if it was happening. His father and one of his sisters calling from Vietnam. They were in one of those booths at the post office across the street from the market. There were two phones in the booth, both on the same extension, and the old man was clasping one while his sister was holding the other. It would be just his luck to pick up the phone and hear his sister say, "Listen. Father is here with me. He wants to say some words to you." Then his father, a man with whom he hadn't spoken for twenty years, would hold the phone against his ear in silence until the sister said, "You can speak now." At which point the old man, still unsure about the phone, would take another moment of silence as if preparing to speak into a tape recorder. My father's throat goes dry as he imagines his father licking his lips and then swallowing before the old man finally speaks, letting out in just one breath all the heat and the dust of that place; the creaking bicycles; the sound of flip-flops slapping against the road; the old women walking to evening mass; the hawkers at the market; the meager shade in the narrow alleys winding toward his childhood home; the Buddhist monks in their robes, crossing the temple courtyard; the smell of the river; the cemetery filled with red earth and seashells piled high as hills; all this would come coursing through the wires and it would enter his body like a riot of blood.

My father lay absolutely still until the phone stopped ringing and the dog stopped jumping. Then he could sit up and get out of bed and walk into the kitchen and pour himself a glass of water and drink it desperately, as though it were a reprieve.

I am trying to take a nap when I hear my mother and my grandfather arguing. My grandfather says, "What would you have had me do, leave him on the beach?" "No," my mother says, "I didn't say that." My grandfather says, "You can't worry about what the women said. They weren't even there. What do they know?" "Some of them were there," my mother says. "And they did nothing but watch," my grandfather says. He adds, "They've frightened you." "Yes," my mother says, her voice barely a whisper.

It stays quiet for a while and then my mother asks, "Was he heavy?" My grandfather sighs and I picture his forehead furrowing. "Yes," he says. And then, "No." And then, "I don't remember." My mother, now talking only to herself, says, "He couldn't have been heavy. He was just a little boy. It was the water, wasn't it? It was the water. The water was heavy."

In Linda Vista, the phone wouldn't stop ringing. Though my father didn't feel he could answer it, he also didn't feel he could disconnect it. He decided to leave the house.

My father packed his reels, rods, and tackles into the back of his gardening truck and drove across the Coronado Bridge, admiring how it arched high over the harbor. He took a right turn off of the bridge, past the rich old houses, past the small beach with its empty swing set, toward a series of piers, pulling into a parking space near a sign that read: IT IS ILLEGAL TO FISH HERE. He understood the English; he knew what it meant, that circle with the line drawn through it of a man holding a fishing pole. But if the police came, he would say, "No know." And they would wag their fingers at him and say, "That's right: No, no." Then he would leave. Until then, he would stay by the piers.

Some nights he didn't bother to get out of the truck. He would drive up, park, sit, and stare at the black water. On the nights he did fish, he found himself holding the pole in his hand as if it weren't a pole but another hand.

He parked the truck and, lighting a cigarette, walked to the end of the nearest pier. He leaned against a post and looked across the water at the lights of the city. More than twenty years ago, he'd stepped off an airplane at the airport downtown and hadn't gone far from the city since. The farthest he'd gone was to Tijuana, where his wife used to buy mangoes and smuggle them across the border in her pocketbook. That was years ago.

When he thought of those early days in the city, he remembered the blinding white light of the sun shining off the sidewalks and the odd grace of the tall palm trees that lined the length of many roads. The bright white light of those days always reminded him that though they couldn't see it, they were all living close to the desert.

From his place at the edge of the pier, he looked across the water at the lights of the city. He saw the neon lights of the business districts, the pale white lights of the streetlamps downtown, the amber lights of residential areas.

Flowing across the bridge were the white headlights and red taillights of cars. The small bursts of light from planes flying overhead looked like stars crawling across the sky. From where he stood, the darkest thing about the city was the water at his feet.

He snuffed out the cigarette against the post, rubbing the ash into the wood. He walked back to the truck, climbed inside and turned the truck toward the bridge. As he pulled out of the parking lot he heard the fishing poles roll across the truck bed. He turned the radio on and listened.

It seemed a lot of noise and a lot of crying, for a boy who was probably watching all this and laughing into his hands. He was laughing at us, at the people dressed in white, with white sashes tied around our heads. He was laughing at the incense smoke that kept blowing into my face and stinging my eyes. He was laughing at the nettles we had to step around as we made our way toward the hole the uncles had dug. He was laughing at the drone of the priest's voice.

My brother could see me standing there, beside my mother. He saw her pull me close to her body and press my head against her hip. When I tried to squirm away, she grabbed my hand and wouldn't let go. I turned back and forth, swinging from her hand, squirming until she had me by just a few fingers. I was on my knees, on the soft red dirt of that ground. I didn't care that my white clothes were getting dirty; I needed to get my hand loose so I could run among the gravestones and see which one he was hiding behind. I wouldn't tag him when I found him; I'd hit him hard. But my mother bent down with me; she wouldn't let go of my hand.

What my brother found funnier than anything else was when one of the women said, "Careful now, the little girl's wild; she'll fall into the hole." My grandfather, glaring at the woman, lifted me from the ground and brought me high up into his arms, managing to keep me there.

My father turned the truck onto Market Street. He was still a couple of blocks from the restaurant where my mother worked, but he decided he would park the truck and walk. It was midnight and the street was mostly empty, though as he walked by the doorways of the closed shops, he noticed the huddled shapes and acrid smells of the people sleeping. On the sidewalk outside San Diego's Finest Copy Store he saw a big cardboard box. It had once held a Xerox copier and now someone's legs were sticking out from one end of it. A young couple made their way toward him. They were drunk. They leaned against each other and, laughing the laugh of drunks—that laugh so close to tears—slowly wound their way past him and disappeared around a corner.

He turned onto the street where my mother worked. It

was part of a historic quarter and lined with tall street-lamps modeled on the old-fashioned gas lamps. He saw her leaning against the stop sign on the corner. She was looking at the ground. The streetlamp cast a pool of light, the very edge of which fell at my mother's feet. As he got closer, Ba saw that she was gazing at the light, as if considering whether to step into it.

One afternoon, more than twenty years ago, they had released him from the reeducation camp. He was dropped off near the church beside Highway One. He walked over to the cyclo drivers who were parked on the corner, under the shade of some tamarind trees, and introduced himself. They let out a cry and threw their arms in the air and apologized. They had not recognized him. Maybe it was because he was so thin or because something in his face had changed or perhaps it was because all their memories were blasted. They made a big show of offering him a cigarette and he accepted. He stood with them and shared a smoke in silence. Then he walked the short distance to his father-in-law's house.

He had never gotten along with his in-laws and was not looking forward to seeing them. They adored their daughter and thought him beneath her. Even now, after years of marriage and all this time apart, they could not stand the fact of her having chosen him.

As he walked, the sound of his flip-flops digging into

the hot sand of the road—a road so close to the water that he always thought of it more as a beach than a road—was like the sound of his voice when he introduced himself to the cyclo drivers: gravelly, parched. He couldn't wait to change out of his clothes, to shed them with the entire war and the years since, like a useless skin. The boy was dead. He needed to remind himself that his son was dead and so not to look for him. Or ask for him. Or blame the sea.

As he neared the entrance to his father-in-law's house, he heard the chickens clucking. He pushed the thatched gate open and stood at the edge of the courtyard. My mother heard the gate brush against the low wall. She came out to see who it was.

Ma stood in the doorway of the house, staring at my father in disbelief. To the side of the house, I stood gazing intently into the family well. I was so engrossed in what I was doing that I hadn't heard my father arrive.

I stood leaning over the mouth of the well. The stillness of my body led Ba to understand that I had just lost something in the water, something I could not see much less retrieve.

My father approached my mother on the street corner. When she looked up she found his expression odd. "Are you all right?" she asked. He nodded, but the expression remained. She couldn't decide which it was: a look of pain or of trouble.

They walked back to the truck in silence.

She saw the fishing poles in the truck bed and noticed that the two white buckets he kept his catch in were empty. Inside the truck, she turned to him and, before she could say anything, he said, "I was going to go fishing. I drove over to Coronado . . ." Shaking his head, he left the sentence unfinished. "Did the police come for you?" she asked. "No," he said. "I got there and then decided to come back." He asked if it had been busy at the restaurant and when she said that it had been, he suggested she nap in the car.

She closed her eyes. It wasn't that she was tired. Looking at him tonight made her anxious.

When the women whispered among themselves that my brother had been swallowed by the sea, I pictured the sea rising in one huge wave, like one of the sheets on my grandmother's clothesline made wild by the wind, and engulfing him. But when the women said, "What happened was, he jumped between two boats—" the wild wave disappeared, my grandmother's sheets settled on the line, and I pictured, very simply, two familiar boats. They were my grandfather's boats. "It was like this," the women said. "The boy jumped from boat to boat." I saw my brother flying through the air. "He must have slipped," the women said. "That must have been what happened. He must have slipped and fallen between the two boats—" "And hit his head—" "The water dragged—" I thought of the shadow of the beached fishing boats, lying half in the sand, half in the water. We would press our bodies against the hull of the boats and run home smelling of salt and sand. "He plunged straight down," the women said, "into a hole in the water."

In my imagination, the hole became a room and the room was in a house, a house exactly like the one I was lying in, playing with shells my grandfather had given me, except that it was underwater. It was darker in my brother's house than it was in mine—and colder—and fish instead of chickens crowded the courtyard.

As the women continued talking about "the boy" and "the bad water," I saw my brother rolling and turning with the tides. I knew him. He was stubborn. I knew that he would continue to do this: he would roll and turn, until, like the shells my grandfather had given me, shells my brother had wanted for himself, shells that had been stripped by the sea of all their markings, his body became as smooth and brilliant as polished bone.

My brother floated across his underwater courtyard, glowing, knowing that in time he would not fade at all; he would only shine brighter.

I wanted him to come back, but I too was stubborn. I hid the shells in my hand. I thought, if need be, I could wait forever. The shells were mine.

. . .

My father parked the truck outside the apartment building. The little white dog started barking as soon as it heard them pull up. As my parents climbed the stairs to their apartment, they heard the tailor's husband in the apartment below mumbling about how noisy the neighborhood had gotten.

My mother felt that living in the building was like living in a village. People communicated to each other by standing at their windows or doorways and talking out loud. When they met in the courtyard or at the local Vietnamese supermarket, they never mentioned anything they'd said or heard. My parents knew that until being told, both the tailor and her husband would pretend not to know my parents had gotten a little white dog. An old woman living alone in the downstairs corner apartment liked to sit at her window and complain about her grown children. They came to visit only once or twice a week. They didn't bother to take off their shoes when they came in. Their children ran around and spoke only English. They talked to her as if she were old and blind but she could see that her daughter-in-law wore too much makeup. A young man living alone in one of the center apartments had started a small herb garden in a long rectangular planter outside his kitchen window. After work, he liked to talk to his girlfriend on the cordless phone while he watered the plants. No one in the building had ever seen the girlfriend and once a neighbor standing at the window had shouted down to him, "How come she never visits?" The young man cradled the phone against his ear, held the water hose with one hand and waved the question away with the other.

It was known that my parents had a daughter who lived on the East Coast, somewhere near New York. Some people heard that she had run away and some people heard that she had simply gone away. That was many years ago and now the rumor was she was writing stories. No one had read them and no one had met her. They imagined that her English was very good.

When I stopped looking for my brother, I began to feel that he was right beside me. So close, I couldn't see him. I imagined everything that was happening to me was also happening to him. When I had a rotten tooth, he had a rotten tooth. When I made friends with a stray dog, my brother approved. When I took naps with our grandfather, holding on to his right arm, my brother held on to his left one. When I walked with my mother to the market, my brother ran ahead of us, weaving his way through the crowd. When my father sang at night and I danced in the courtyard, my mother said, "Stop dancing with your shadow." But I was dancing with my brother.

Everywhere I went in our town my brother went with me, but when I left for America, I left him sleeping with my grandfather on the low wooden bed by the window. Years passed and my grandfather's arms grew into sinuous vines, wrapping the house in leaves and brambles. Inside the house, my brother and my grandfather fell into a deep sleep.

Outside the thatched gate of our house in Vietnam, life went on. Up and down the street, the women laid out trays of small silver fish to dry. The bodies of the fish glinted like small broken mirrors. At night, the squid boats dotted the horizon. In the morning, the women carried the fishermen's catch to the market. In the spring, firecrackers were lit to celebrate the New Year. When the rains came, the cyclo drivers pedaled laboriously through the mud. Schoolboys played soccer on the town beach in the late afternoons while a young girl made her way between the bathers, offering small bags of boiled peanuts to anyone who would buy them.

My mother walked through the apartment, turning all the lights on. Though it was now a quarter to one in the morning, after a long night of cooking at the restaurant, she didn't feel like going to sleep. She walked into the bedroom and put her pocketbook away, under the mattress. My father turned on the television in the living room and followed my mother into the bedroom. The little dog followed my father. My mother came out of the bedroom, turned the television off, and walked into the kitchen. She filled a small pot with water and put it on the stove to boil. She chopped some ginger and threw it in the pot to simmer. Her stomach felt jumpy and she thought the ginger tea might help. My father came out of the bedroom wearing his sleeping clothes: a San Diego Chargers T-shirt and loose sweatpants. He turned on the television and walked into the kitchen. "Are you making tea?" he asked. My mother nodded, walking by him on her way into the bedroom.

While she showered, he watched the television. The sound was off but it didn't matter; a weather map was on the monitor. First it showed their region, and then it showed the entire country. "Sunshine," my father said, out loud. Then, reading off the monitor, "Highs. Lows." When he heard the shower turn off, he walked into the kitchen and strained the tea into two glasses. The little dog ran through the kitchen, out to the patio. My father filled a glass with water and poured it into the dog's water bowl.

In the bedroom, my mother put on the slip-dress she liked to sleep in. It was cream-colored with a blue trim around the hem. She had bought the dress at a department store in Tijuana years ago. At the border crossing on the way back to the U.S., she used the dress to cover some mangoes she had hidden at the bottom of her purse. When they got home that day, and she pulled the dress out of her purse, it smelled of mangoes. She told my father and he raised his eyebrows and said, "What a delicious dress!"

My mother sat on the edge of the bed and combed her hair. She heard my father turning out the lights in the other rooms. She put the comb down on the dresser and climbed into bed.

When we first came to America, my mother used to save money and send it home to her family in Vietnam. She'd roll the bills in squares of tinfoil and hide them in tubes of toothpaste. Along with the money, she sent home soaps, headache tablets, asthma pumps, bolts of cloth, shampoos and conditioners. She explained to me that times were hard "over there"; my aunts could sell the goods on the black market to get some extra money.

I imagined my aunts using all the money to hire horsemen who they hoped could charge the thatched gate and tear through the bramble to wake my grandfather and my brother. Team after team of horsemen had attempted the journey but none had made it past the gate that I, sitting an ocean away, guarded so closely. Chickens and roosters, stray dogs and the stench of dried fish did my bidding; in my absence, they kept the horsemen back.

.   .   .

My father walked into the bedroom carrying a glass of ginger tea in each hand. He handed the glasses to my mother and got into bed beside her. They sat up in bed sipping their tea and talking. She asked him what he'd done that day. He said, "Not much, actually. I mostly watched the news." "What was in the news?" she asked.

What immediately came to mind was the image of the woman in the blue kerchief, standing in the field of green grass. He had considered that image all day and it had taken him the entire day to understand that the woman had been crying. Every time the camera came back to her, she shook her head and pointed to the ground. When the camera shot the ground, all he had seen was a lush field. As lush as a rice paddy, he remembered thinking. Now he had a feeling that the woman was pointing to bodies, unseen bodies, under the grass. As she directed the eye of the camera back to the grass, she kept crying because of what it could not see and what she could not stop seeing.

My father turned to my mother and instead of telling her about the woman, he talked about the weather. He said, "There was a wildfire outside L.A. and a flood in the middle of the country." "What else?" my mother asked.

"I don't know," my father said. "I turned the sound off after that." She looked disappointed so he said, "I know that tomorrow a Santa Ana blowing in from the desert will bring snow showers." She smiled. "Tomorrow the mayor honors all Vietnamese women in the San Diego area, especially the Vietnamese women living in the neighborhood of Linda Vista who also happen to be married to gardeners." "That's everyone!" she said. "In celebration," my father continued, "the mayor says, 'Free pho for everyone!' " "And who will cook it?" my mother asked. "I guess the gardeners," my father said.

My mother laughed. She said, "Anh . . ." and kissed my father goodnight.

When I approached the entrance to my childhood home, there were no brambles to step around or tangled vines to cut through. There was no longer a thatched gate to push open or chickens to keep inside. I crossed the heat of the courtyard. A dog that had recently given birth to sand-colored puppies eyed me suspiciously from a corner of the front porch. I climbed the two steps leading up to the house. At the doorway, I took off my shoes. When I stepped into the shade of the inside, the coolness of the tile floor against my bare foot was like stepping into a pool of water.

. . .

I don't know how time moves or which of our sorrows or our desires it is able to wash away. I return after twenty years still expecting my brother to step out of the sea. Though I'm taken to the cemetery the first day back, no part of me believes he is actually beneath the light blue plaster headstone. His name, the years of his birth and his death, all etched in red, do not identify him to me in any way. Walking along the streets and among the market stalls, I half expect to turn and find him, a young man moving along beside me, someone whose face I may no longer recognize but whose body my body will recall.

I can't sleep. If he was here, I'd press my head against his belly, the two of us like dogs sleeping through the heat of midday.

I went to the town beach. In the early morning, the water was calm. I could stand in it up to my shoulders and lay my palms on the surface to feel the sea rippling beneath my fingertips like the fabric of a shawl. In the late afternoon, the wind picked up, drawing gusts of sand down the beach, like a transparent curtain behind which the waves were wildly dancing.

I sat and watched as the schoolboys kicked their soccer ball from one end of the beach to the other. Sometimes the ball rolled so languidly, it seemed there was no goal to the game, but then the ball would be driven in just a few seconds, in a direct line, down the beach, or kicked so high into the air that when it landed, it made a hard sound, as of something heavy having fallen.

Waking in a sweat in the middle of the night and unable to fall back to sleep, I left the house and walked down to the water. With the squid boats bobbing in the distance before me and the sleeping town at my back, I swam straight out, as fast and as far as I could go, my body rocking from side to side, my arms arcing through the air, my hands cutting into the dark water.

My father glanced over at the clock on the dresser—4:35. Beside him, my mother was fast asleep. He hadn't been able to sleep for the past couple of hours, had been trying to lie as still as possible so as not to disturb her, but now he decided to get up. Slowly, he turned onto his side and rolled out of the bed. Quietly, he left the bedroom and walked out to the living room. The little white dog was asleep on the couch. When my father walked by, it lifted its head to look but didn't follow. He went into the kitchen and poured himself a glass of water. He carried a chair out to the side porch and sat down. He drank the water and looked up at the moon. It hung like a hammock in the sky. He thought about my mother, on her feet all night. He was glad to know she was sleeping now.

He leaned back in his chair, put his feet against the wall and thought about her feet. Lines from a poem he used to recite to her when they had first met now returned to him.

In the poem, a man says that if he could marry the woman he loves, he would pull the moon out of the sky and turn it into a pool for her to wash her feet in. My father recited what he could remember of the poem quietly to himself, pleased to note how familiar it sounded, like an old song.

He took another sip of water and sat listening to the night's sounds. Crickets hummed under the juniper bushes on the edge of the driveway. A car with a bad ignition was chugging along Linda Vista Road. The face of the woman he'd seen on television—the one who had been pointing at the ground—came back to him. He thought about how when he had first seen the woman, standing in the field of grass, it was the color of the grass, that bright green of new spring leaves, that caught his attention. But now, when he thought of the news clip, he could see only the woman herself, shaking her head and pointing away. "Don't look at me," she seemed to be saying with her head and eyes and hands.

My father thought the woman would not be able to rest until she had dug, with her own bare hands, through that field. He pictured her, on her hands and knees, slowly making her way. Like a gardener, she would feel for everything with her fingertips, sometimes caressing what her hands came across, gently shaking the soil loose from the roots, at other times pulling up in one motion what needed to be torn away.

Thinking of the bright green field she stood in, he

remembered the bodies that floated through the rice paddies during the war. All those badly buried bodies. What happened to such bodies?

Sitting on his porch in Linda Vista he thought about loading all his gardening equipment into his truck. He would drive to wherever she was and offer her his help, his hands.

Above him, the moon continued to cast its light. He said the word "moon" aloud, in English. Often when he said a word in English, he would think of how his daughter might say it.

One night, during our first spring together in California, my father woke my mother and me and told us to grab our coats and put on our shoes. He wanted to show us something. When Ma reached for her pocketbook, Ba said that she wouldn't need it, but she brought it anyway, clasping it under her arm.

Ba drove us to the beach. We got out of the car and he led us toward the sea. At first, there seemed to be nothing but that long familiar expanse of darkness. We'd seen it before; it was the open sea, late at night, with no one around.

As we walked toward the water, I noticed that in the silence following each wave's crash scattered sparks of light appeared across the sand.

The beach was covered with small silver fish whose bodies gave off a strange light. The fish made their way toward us, turning their backs and baring their bellies to the full moon. They writhed in the wet sand and it seemed that the more they writhed, the brighter they became. Up close, their little mouths moved busily, as if they could not get enough of the cool salt night air.

Out from the darkness of the sea, wave after wave of small, luminous bodies washed to shore.

My father turned to my mother and me and, smiling broadly, pointed at the fish, as if we knew them.

My father remembers stroking my mother's face.
My mother remembers wearing my father's coat.
I remember taking off my sandals and digging my heels into the wet sand.

As my parents stood on the beach leaning into each other, I ran, like a dog unleashed, toward the lights.

acknowledgments

Grateful acknowledgments are offered to the following:

The Lê's of Linda Vista—Minh, Thin, Trinh, Van, and Danny.

Corita Brown, Tadd Fernée, Cheli Morales, and Cassidy O'Laughlin Richey—friends from the start.

Tish Allan, Julie Fernée, Lynne Hanley, Carla Kirkwood, and Nina Payne—for their early support and encouragement.

Anna Grace, Margaret Kilgallen, Marjorie Gellhorn Sa'adah, and Lisa Schlesinger—for conversations along the way.

George Andreou and Ursula Doyle—in whose capable hands I was fortunate to find myself.

Nicole Aragi—who risked a speeding ticket to find me and then waited most patiently, and with great faith.

Special thanks to Peter Simpson who—time and again— gave me refuge.

· · ·

The author would like to thank the Headlands Center for the Arts, Hedgebrook, the Lannan Foundation, and Jeffrey Farrell and Bruno Boussière for providing residencies where portions of this book were written.

a note about the author

lê thi diem thúy was born in Phan Thiet, southern Vietnam. She and her father left Vietnam in 1978, by boat, eventually settling in southern California. thúy lê currently resides in western Massachusetts.

a note on the type

Pierre Simon Fournier le jeune, who designed the type used in this book, was both an originator and a collector of types. His services to the art of printing were his design of letters, his creation of ornaments and initials, and his standardization of type sizes. His types are old style in character and sharply cut. In 1764 and 1766 he published his *Manuel typographique*, a treatise on the history of French types and printing, on type-founding in all its details, and on what many consider his most important contribution to typography—the measurement of type by the point system. Composed by Creative Graphics, Inc., Allentown, Pennsylvania. Printed and bound by R. R. Donnelley and Sons, Harrisonburg, Virginia. Designed by Iris Weinstein.